Caution in the Wind

Book Two: The Treasure Seekers

a novel

by

William N. Gilmore

William N. Gilmore

First Printing

Book design by William N. Gilmore
Cover art by Heather Trim of TrimVentures Media
www.TrimVentures.com

ISBN:978-1-946689-02-3

Manufactured by Kindle Direct Publishing

www.kdp.amazon.com

Printed in the United States of America

Caution in the Wind

Book Two: The Treasure Seekers

William N. Gilmore

Books

by

William N. Gilmore

Caution in the Wind

Book One: Partnerships

Books in the Larry Gillam and Sam Lovett

Detective Series

Book One:

BLUE BLOODS & BLACK HEARTS

Book Two:

GOLD BADGES & DARK SOULS

Book Three:

BLUE KNIGHTS & WHITE LIES

Other Books:

Saints, Sinners, Lovers and Others

Poems and Prose

From Thoughts That Arose

No Space For Justice

Acknowledgements

As always, I first have to give a big thank you to my wife, Esther. Together we've shared fun adventures at home and out west.

We've been witnesses to some remarkable things; we've seen the beauty in our own country, massive red oak trees, high waterfalls, and mountains so majestic they would make you cry; new growth right after a devastating forest fire; mountains of snow from the winter falls still closing roads in the summer; a newly born fawn trying to cross a paved road with its mother, unsure of its footing on the strange surface for the first time; an eagle diving into a lake to catch a fish larger than itself, trying to take flight with its catch and not drown; ghost towns with real ghosts of soiled doves who like to play dirty tricks; the look on a young grandson's face seeing a geyser shoot two-hundred feet into the air, and eating a huckleberry for the first time; watching our grandson grow and seeing his first child being born.

We've seen a lot of history and maybe even made a little too, so Esther, thank you, I love you, and I look forward to continuing this wonderful adventure with you.

To my entire family. I love you all.

To the Paulding County Writers' Guild. I can't thank you guys enough for everything. The friendship, the support, the ideas, and the critiques; the good and the not so good.

To my readers. Thank you. I hope you will continue to enjoy and support my work.

To the mountain men, trappers, guides, prospectors, explorers, and soldiers who were the first non-natives to see the vast wonders, carving the paths for so many others to follow.

To the brave men, women, and children who took the new trails to the West to start new lives, find riches, settle the land, and find adventure.

To the many who did not survive the harsh environments of the trip and whose graves, marked and unmarked, litter the entire stretch between the trailheads and the West from disease, accidents, drownings, suicides, lack of water, food, or medicines, hostile Indians, cutthroats, childbirths, and trying their best.

To those who keep us safe and sacrifice themselves so others won't have to. We salute you. We thank you.

WNG

Still Remembering

My Friend Mike

This is not a history book. This is a work of fiction, of course, however, I have strived to make it as accurate as possible with my research on the emigrant movement to the West in 1850; the people, their struggles, the equipment, the routes, and even the land itself.

I am not a historian and I don't pretend to be. I am sure there are mistakes, omissions, inaccuracies, flubs, and screw-ups in my telling of this story.

What I want is to give you a very entertaining and pleasurable reading experience, partly based on historical facts from historical records, journals, family Bibles, genealogical records, and tall tales, some of it told with a bit of license.

Also, I have used my experience and knowledge as an Atlanta Police Detective (retired) in my research.

I hope you will look on this as a continuing fun, exciting, informative, and captivating story, and will allow me to be your next favorite author (if I'm not already).

Please, hold onto your hat and enjoy this adventure.

WNG

CHAPTER 1

Darkness.

William N. Gilmore

CHAPTER 2

It was the middle of 1840 when Joseph Long finally began the long voyage home. He was nearing the end of the most important mission of his life. He was nervous, scarcely able to eat or sleep, walking the entire ship at all hours, constantly checking the hold where the precious cargo was secured.

It was a mission of such great importance, full of deep secrets and dire consequences, he feared using his real name. When asked, he presented expertly forged papers identifying him as a merchant of industrial goods.

Accompanying him on the voyage home were sealed containers marked as tools, printing machines, and other such goods destined for the young country far across the waves; the United States of America.

The truth was that hidden within many of these sealed boxes and barrels were gold coins and bullion provided by the British monarchs in support of the growing abolitionist movement in those United States. However, it was without the approval or even the knowledge of Parliament.

The new Liberty Party was leading the anti-slavery political agenda and at its first national convention in April of 1840, was trying to nominate a candidate to run for President of the United States, but they needed financial backing for their movement. A lot of it.

England, not wanting to look as if it were trying to influence the U.S. national election, made the contribution of nearly a million British Pounds in gold from the Royal Mint in secret. All the gold sovereigns and half sovereigns already minted for 1840 but not having been released by the mint, to include all the bullion, which was delegated for the minting of those coins, was given to Long.

The deal was intended to be kept secret by concealing all transactions and destroying all documents. The Crown also provided an unregistered ship and a special crew to deliver Long and his 'goods' to a pre-arraigned rendezvous with agents on the United States East Coast.

Only a handful of people knew about the ship they were to meet, but not what it carried. A strict timetable was set, and it should have arrived on their second day of waiting. However, all during that time, there were storms and gales. After four days, they sent one of their members back for instructions. After five, two others left; miserable, wet, and getting sick. After seven days, the one who left for instructions returned only to find there was now no one to give them to. He left before the end of the eighth day, returning with the unsettling news; Joseph Long and the ship were surely lost, wrecked, or in the hands of another.

James G. Birney, the presidential candidate from the

Liberty Party did not receive the financial backing he and the party so desperately needed. He lost handily. The Kentuckian, himself a former slaveholder, was nominated again for the 1844 election, but once again he lost. However, he took votes which may have kept Henry Clay from the high office, giving the win to James Polk.

Joseph Long was never heard from again, and the ship, well, the ship went down quickly with all hands. Or, so it was believed. One lone survivor somehow managed to get away through the storm which took the ship and his associates to the bottom. He washed up on shore, badly bruised with several broken bones and a severe head injury. He languished for several days until he was found by a young girl searching the beach for clams.

He was taken to her home where she tried to care for him while waiting for a doctor from another village, but he was in too bad a shape and didn't last long. However, during one of the few times he appeared lucid, he told his young, caring nurse about the ship, Long, and the gold. How their mission might keep the country from dividing over the most debated of social issues and possibly keep the country from a great civil war.

He told young Esther how during the violent storm, the cargo broke free in the hold, causing the ship to list and take on water. He was one of Long's security men and closest aides, and one of the few to know all the details of the secret mission. He was ordered to try and secure the secret cargo below deck with other crew members before it became apparent what they were carrying.

Heavy boxes and barrels were now loose in the hold being thrown against the inside hull triggering damage allowing the forceful water to come rushing in. One of the many boxes labeled as tools broke open to reveal hundreds of gold coins. They were now scattered throughout the belly of the hold.

Many of the crew foolishly abandoned their work in the hold and tried to grab as much of the gold for themselves, putting the coins in their pockets or shirts. They were blinded by the gold and never made it out of the ship when it capsized. It went down quickly in almost one piece.

After a few days of suffering, the poor man died without giving any further information and was buried in a small, nearby cemetery. Esther never knew his name, where he was from, or if he left any family behind. She didn't know if during the time he was delirious, he was telling a made-up story, or if the tale he told could somehow be real.

Esther never told anyone of the man's alleged confession or his wild, mesmerizing story until she told her husband, Patrick Murphy, many years later.

CHAPTER 3

The California and Oregon Trails were a combination of several trails which began at jumping-off points on the Missouri River. Independence and St. Joseph were just two of the main trailheads. Further along the journey, the trails would split for groups going to their final destinations such as the Oregon Territory, the Utah Territory, or the California gold fields.

Some trails were safer or less rugged than others, some were shorter but there were the dangers of hostile Indians or shortages of where to find water and grass for livestock.

The weather was also a major consideration. You better make it over the mountainous trails before the big snows came, or across the long, foreboding deserts before the rains or the heat took hold. The sands could swallow you up and the winds could tear the skin from your bones.

Along many of the trails, there were markers of the dead. Those who died of accident, attacks, or more likely, disease. Too many were children.

There were nearly a hundred wagons in the group Patrick and Mike joined. They were required to sign a contract with the wagon master outlining the many rules and conditions.

There was a vote among the travelers for captain and

lieutenants who would be responsible for maintaining order and for protection of the party. A scout would travel ahead every day to find the best locations to cross rivers, camp, and hopefully, finding water and grass for the animals.

Dust. No one warned Patrick and Mike just how bad it would be. It wasn't in the books they bought. It didn't take long for them to figure it out though. They learned for themselves to stay back from any wagons in front of them or to put a handkerchief or some other like covering over their noses and mouths.

At least it wasn't mud which could have been a hundred times worse. Some wagons could sink all the way up to their hubs, and animals would not be able to move forward at all. This was another reason to keep the wagons as light as possible.

The sucking mud would pull your boots off while trying to push and you'd be wearing it all day and maybe all night or longer. And you better hope you got your wagon out before it dried. On a good day, you might make three whole miles through the mess. It took a toll on both the travelers and their animals.

They would learn many more little lessons along the trail, like making butter by placing milk in a covered bucket or other container and letting the rough jostling of the wagon do the churning, or if you could get them, spacing eggs in the flower barrel so they wouldn't break while driving over the rough trails.

The first few days went very well, averaging about fifteen

miles a day. No wagons broke down, but a few which were overburdened fell behind. They were warned by the wagon master and told the rest of the group would not be held up for only one or two wagons.

Sometimes, large families or groups traveling together would have several wagons and if one developed a problem, they would all stop to help. It would be their responsibility to catch up, turn around, or join another party. Now, with so many headed for the California gold fields, there was usually one just a couple of days behind and it wasn't uncommon for more than one wagon train to be at a rest stop at a time.

It didn't take long before some travelers finding themselves falling behind unloaded heavy, unnecessary items such as iron stoves, organs and pianos, metal bed frames, and other such luxuries. Many of these items ended up being left on the side of the trail for scavengers.

Most of the travelers walked a majority of the trip beside their wagons. The wagons were not a comfortable ride anyway and again, they wanted to keep them as light as possible so as not to wear out the animals pulling the load. Shoes were reshod for the animals and resoled for the people many times over during the months-long journey.

The day would begin before sunrise. First breakfast, then feed the animals and get them harnessed to the wagons so everyone was off at first light. The day would end oppositely;

stopping while there was still light, getting the wagons into a formation for protection and to corral the animals inside, doing chores of maintaining the wagons, feeding the animals, collecting firewood or buffalo chips, and getting dinner ready.

Several guards would be put out every night on a rotating shift to guard the wagons and the herds. Usually two to four hours. Once in a while, someone would claim to see something or fire a shot which would wake most everyone.

The many different languages spoken was also a problem at times. Many German-speaking persons and other immigrants did not speak any or at best, spoke awfully bad English. This caused several problems including mistrust, prejudice, misunderstanding, and more than a few fights.

When the captain and his lieutenants tried to settle any disagreements, more times than not, it became a shouting match no one could understood.

One lady from a large church group traveling together held school-like classes whenever the wagons stopped for the night. She was a teacher and taught English for children and adults alike by firelight.

The grueling days, the hot sun, and the tired muscles made for a truly short evening in most cases. Once the chores were done and the animals were taken care of, dinner and then a few hours of sleep was the next order of business just so you could get up early and do it all over again the next day.

CHAPTER 4

Caution was surrounded by darkness. She was a little groggy still and her nose hurt. She remembered the men in the blue uniforms who came out of the house and into the backyard. Molly didn't like them. She got between Caution and the men as they approached. She growled and barked even after she was told to stop. Molly knew things just were not right.

When one of the men got close enough to grab Caution, Molly jumped up and grabbed him by his arm. The man yelled out with pain and tried to knock Molly loose. Caution tried to run, but the other man caught her quickly. She heard Molly snarling and the man screaming out bad words as he fell to the ground.

The man who held Caution carried her over to the other man just as he put a cloth over her nose and mouth. He kicked at Molly and she heard her cry out, then nothing. Caution struggled as she tried to breathe. She was being forced to breathe through the damp and funny smelling cloth. Something was causing her to get dizzy until she couldn't struggle any more. Everything went dark.

Caution awoke with something over her head, maybe a cloth bag or hood, and tape around her hands and feet, and over her mouth. She could breathe, but she couldn't see. By the way it felt, she believed she was in a big cardboard box, but she wasn't sure. It didn't have much room. She could barely move around or shake it, but with just a little effort, she was able to sit up.

The wooziness was nearly all gone. She was scared. She felt like crying. Then, she remembered more. *Did they hurt Molly? Was she alright? Mother? Mother was in the house. Did they hurt Mother before they came after me?* Caution struggled with trying to loosen the bonds around her hands, but they were too tight. Now, she was mad.

There was a sudden loss of balance as she was thrust to one side of the box. She realized she was in a moving vehicle and it just made a turn. She believed she was in a truck or van and the motion made her believe she was facing towards the back of the vehicle.

She didn't have any idea how long she may have been in the box, or the vehicle, and she wasn't able to track all of its movements. She knew no one was going to know where she was. She began to get scared all over again.

She wished her Grandpa Patrick was with her. She didn't think he would be able to do much, but it would make her feel better. *What would Detective Winston—Vickie do?* she thought. *She would stay calm and do her detective stuff. She's smart and brave. I have to be the same. Vickie will figure it out and find me. I just have to have faith.*

Before long, the vehicle stopped and seemed to be backing up and stopped again. She thought she heard muffled voices and then heard what sounded like a big, metal door being pulled down. A few seconds later, other doors open, maybe to the back of the vehicle. The voices were a little louder now.

The box was being jostled a bit, then she could tell it was being lifted slightly and tilted. There was movement again and she believed she was being taken off the vehicle, but where? "Help me with this thing will you," one of the voices was saying, "she's heavy and my left arm ain't working so good. The bandages are too tight. Did you have to kick the stupid dog in the head while my arm was in its teeth?"

"You're lucky I was able to get it off at all," another voice responded. "Her little dog was making hamburger out of you. Good thing there was a first aid kit in this van, it took all the gauze and tape to patch you up and keep you from bleeding all over me. You're welcome by the way."

"You think it might have rabies or something?"

"I doubt it, they're rich. I'm sure they took it for its shots," he said. "Put her down here."

Caution felt the forward motion stop, the box level out, and a jarring thump as it met with the floor. She knew not to make any movement or sound. She listened. That's what Vickie would do.

"You think she's awake yet?"

"I don't know. Does it matter?"

"I don't want to have to deal with a crying, snotty kid. I think it was a mistake taking her. We should have taken the woman instead."

"It's wasn't your call. He wanted the kid."

"Okay, we got her. Now what?"

"We wait for orders, so shut up and relax."

"When do we get paid?"

"When the job is done."

"When do we eat?"

"You're a pain, you know that? You go and bring me something back too. Bring something for the kid. We don't know how long we'll have to babysit her, and I don't want to hear her whine. Something close so it's still hot. Maybe I'll get some peace and quiet while you're gone. Talk about crying. Keep it up and I'll have to put tape over your mouth too."

"Sheesh, Roger, you don't have to get so nasty about it. Toss me the van keys. I'll be back in just a jiffy.

"Don't be going anywhere else. We don't need some smart cop checking on vans, pulling it over before we clean it out and wipe it down. And don't forget to make my drink a diet soda."

"Diet? That's a laugh," the man said as he twisted his mustache with the hand on his good arm.

"Sure. Don't you know it cancels out whatever you might

eat that would have the same amount of calories as a regular soda?"

"Now you're just being stupid."

"You want me to use the chloroform on you too? Get outa here."

"Okay, okay, I'm goin'."

Caution heard the van start up and begin to drive off, then an overhead door being pulled down. She was gathering information; a little here, a little there. She smiled the best she could under the tape, she believed both Grandpa Patrick and Vickie would be proud of her. It gave her strength. She was right.

William N. Gilmore

CHAPTER 5

Patrick and Mike were walking the perimeter of the circled wagons as late-night security when Mike thought he saw something in the light of the large crescent moon.

Mike, with his new, double-barreled shotgun, brought it up, pointed it out into the night, waving it around.

"What did you see, Mike?" Patrick asked, looking around in the dim light, placing his hand on the grip of his big, holstered pistol.

"I don't bloody know. I think I saw something moving out there. It could be one of those Indians."

"Don't shoot at it," Patrick said, carefully placing his hand on the barrel of Mike's gun and slowly lowering it. "It could be one of the animals got loose, something else, or nothin' at all. Make sure first."

"I don't like it out here in the bloody dark," Mike said.

"It ain't completely dark. The moon be smiling at you."

"It be dark enough. Things come out in the dark."

"Things, what things?" Patrick asked.

"You know. Spirits, elves, and goblins; the bad stuff."

"Those things ain't real. Just stories to scare people."

"And I be one of 'em," Mike admitted. "I heard stories

about bad things coming out in the night and taking the children who were bad and causing mischief and those who done told lies and said vulgar words."

"I was told the same things. I think most children are told things like that to get them to behave or to go to bed when they should."

"What about the Far Darrig?" Mike asked in a hushed voice. "It be for real. It steals normal, beautiful babies and switches them with ugly, stupid ones. I know a few who must have been swapped."

"I think I know one too," Patrick stated.

"See, I told ya," Mike said, not getting the jest.

"Just shut up and keep walking," Patrick insisted. "Keep the hammers down and take your finger off the triggers. Keep your wits about yourself but keep your eyes open." He wasn't sure if Mike really saw something or not but kept his hand on his big pistol the rest of their shift.

During the trip, Patrick and Mike took turns driving the wagon and when not walking, riding on the horse Patrick bought. It was a big, black horse Patrick named Midnight.

Both lacked any real experience with riding and didn't stray far from the wagon until they got better. Patrick and Mike wanted to go hunting with some of the men. Only groups of three or more could go out. No one was allowed to ride off by themselves except for the scout. This was smart in case someone alone got hurt, attacked, lost, or just didn't return for whatever reason.

Big Mike finally got a chance to join a group of men going out to get some fresh meat a couple of hours before the wagons stopped for the day. He saddled up Midnight and grabbed his shotgun with a supply of powder and shot. He hoped to get a deer, but rabbit, squirrel, or a good-sized bird would be more likely.

"Try not to shoot yourself or anyone else," Patrick said, kiddingly, but knew it could happen. "Don't put the caps on until you have a good target."

"I bloody well know what I be doin'," Mike said, sitting on top of Midnight as he rode beside the wagon. "You'll be doin' some skinnin' and cookin' in just a bit when I get back."

Mike rode off to join the five or six men on horseback as they headed off from the wagons. He didn't run the horse as he was still a little unsure of himself and bounced on the animal a little too much.

Just a couple of miles from the wagon train, the hunters found themselves near a wooded area and seeing some tracks, figured they might find some game in the area.

Mike and several of the men dismounted and loaded their rifles. Mike loaded his shotgun, including putting caps on the nipples for both barrels, but keeping the hammers down. One of the men held his shotgun so he could get back up on Midnight, handing it to him once he was ready.

Mike loaded shot for small game, hoping to get something to take back and show Patrick. It wasn't too long before Mike saw a rabbit as it moved through the thicket not too far away. He made sure no one was in danger of getting hit by a possible wild shot and brought his shotgun up. He aimed. He fired.

Midnight reared up, spooked by the loud blast and Mike went tumbling in a backward summersault off the rear of the big horse. Midnight galloped off as two of the other men went after him.

Mike got up brushing himself off, cursing, but relatively unhurt except for his pride. The men snickered after making sure Mike was alright but didn't say anything. He picked up the shotgun thankful the other chamber didn't go off by accident when it hit the ground.

"There be another lesson learned," Mike said, obviously embarrassed. "Don't shoot from the back of a damn thick horse what ain't been bloody well trained not to jump at loud sounds."

Mike walked over towards the thicket hoping for a miracle. "Praise be the Saints!" he exclaimed. There was the rabbit, right where he hoped it would be, shot deader than dirt.

Before long, the other two men returned with Midnight in tow. He still acted a little skittish but allowed Mike to mount him without any problem. He put the rabbit in a bag and tied it to the saddle horn.

"Well," Mike stated, his confidence restored, "let's go. I'm sure this ain't the only critter the good Lord put on this blessed Earth."

They got a few more rabbits, some birds, and some squirrels, and one man said he even got a shot off at a dear but missed. After a couple of hours, they headed back to the wagons.

On a ridge paralleling them some distance away, they saw the outline of several riders moving in the same direction as they were. They kept pace with the hunting party, not bothering to hide. They were Indians. The hunting party picked up the pace a little, now only about a mile from the wagon train.

They made it without any incident but told the captain what they saw. They were told not to tell anyone else; they didn't want to panic any of their group. For the next couple of nights, the guard was doubled.

Of course, Mike told Patrick about witnessing the Indians, but only after showing off his prized rabbit.

William N. Gilmore

CHAPTER 6

Bill and Vickie were shocked and devastated by the news of Caution's abduction. Vickie comforted Mrs. Murphy the best she could, assuring her she would do her best to get Caution back safe and as quickly as possible. She took all the information which was known at the time, taking notes, names, and phone numbers, including those of Special Agent Tommy McGill.

Agent McGill was a little hesitant and standoffish with providing all the information to Detective Winston.

"You're not assigned to this case, are you, detective?" McGill asked.

"Well, not exactly," she responded. "I'm a friend of the family," she said, stretching the truth just a bit. "Plus, I am assigned to a case which may be related; a burglary case."

"Is there a suspect?" Agent McGill asked.

"I tell you what, Agent McGill. I'd love to sit here and go over old cases with you, but there is a little girl out there; scared, alone, and in need of our immediate help. I need to be out there looking for her."

Hearing the brash discussion about Caution, Sean Murphy walked over to the group.

"Vickie," Mr. Murphy interrupted. "Please, both of you;

any information which could help us locate Caution would be vital. I understand you are upset, we all are, but I need you to work with Agent McGill on this and get her back to us, safe and sound. There are no secrets now."

"You're right, Mr. Murphy, I'm sorry, Agent McGill. I let my emotions get the best of me."

"It's understandable, detective. Any information the two of you can provide will be useful. You know how this works."

Bill started with the story about the coin Sam found and going to the coin store where he first encountered Dearing. As he relayed his information, he got to the point about how he was being followed by the private investigator, Gerald Olson who was working for Mr. Murphy.

"Wait. What was that?" Sean asked.

"I know. I didn't get a chance to talk with you about him and his man from last night," Bill said. "I was going to call you and tell you to pull your men, we don't need the protection."

"I'm not sure I understand," Mr. Murphy started. "I didn't give him any instructions to follow you or Detective Winston. He does a few things for me. I keep him on retainer and sometimes if John is doing a dive in a risky location, I have him keep an eye on him."

"Then why was he following me and why was his man watching Vickie?"

"And what about the man I shot last night in my

apartment," Vickie asked. "What is his connection with this?"

"What man?" Both Mr. Murphy and Agent McGill asked at the same time.

Bill and Vickie gave Tommy and Sean all the information on the incident and the identity of the dead guy, Adam Dearing.

Agent McGill ordered up a full investigation into both Dearing's and Olson's backgrounds to include any associates, other relatives, vehicles, addresses, holdings; the whole works.

Mr. Murphy stated he did not know Dearing other than what Bill told him. There was no reason to doubt him in this situation. It was obvious the parents would do anything to get their daughter back.

The Murphy's gave names and telephone numbers of friends and associates, their business dealings, and a list of employees including those who were recently released, denied work, quit, or were fired. The lists would be sent over to the FBI to investigate if there were any connections.

Somewhere, someone knew something, or there was a clue out there waiting to be found. Getting vital information could take some time, something they were afraid they didn't have much of and was closing in on them in a hurry.

*

Caution was trying to be as quiet as possible, listening for anything which might be important. Being in the box with a hood on kept things muffled. She needed to get out if nothing more than to check her immediate surroundings. Be a good detective.

What she knew so far was she was quite sure there were only two men who took her from her home. She wasn't sure how far they may have taken her in what was probably a van. One just left but may be returning soon. His name was unknown, but the one who was with her was named Roger and she was in a building with a big, noisy, pull-down door.

Now it was time to try and get more information. She managed to get her hands up under the hood just enough to pull the tape off her mouth. It hurt and burned a little and made her lips sticky. It tasted bad too. She knew she needed to take a chance, thinking carefully what to do and say.

"Excuse me, mister?" she said as softly and meekly as she could.

There was no answer.

"Mister, hello. Are you there?" she said a little louder.

"Be quiet. You ain't supposed to be talking. Do you want me to put more tape over your mouth?" he said sharply.

"I'm sorry, sir. I need to use the restroom, please." Caution tried to sound pathetic and desperate all at the same time without seeming to be hysterical. "I promise I'll be good."

"You'll need to hold it for a while. Now, be quiet."

"Sir, I've held it real long. I'm afraid I can't any longer. It will be a real mess and stinky in here in just a minute."

"Is the tape still on your hands and feet and do you still have the hood on?" the man asked.

"Yes. I just pulled the tape off my mouth, so I could tell you I needed to go. I won't cause you any problems, I promise."

"If you try to run away or scream, I'll wring your neck, are we clear?"

"Yes, sir, I won't do any of those things."

"No questions, no more talking. You do your business and then it's right back in the box. If you don't do what I say, when I say, you'll regret it. Do you know what I mean?"

"Yes, sir."

Caution felt the box move slightly and heard something at the top. It sounded like the top was being cut open. It took a minute or two, but soon the top was opened. Caution could tell the difference in the light filtering through the hood and felt the cool air come in, surrounding her.

"You keep your hood on or else we'll have to make sure you never go home again, understood?"

"Yes, Sir." Caution knew not to engage the man in conversation or to answer in any other way for now. She knew she would have to play their game until the situation was different. For now, keep it short.

The man helped her out of the box. Caution was a little wobbly on her feet from being both cramped up in the box and being disorientated because of the hood. However, now she was in some light and she could see vague shapes and shadows. He cut the tape around her feet.

The man took her by the arm and walked her for about twenty-five feet until he stopped and opened a door, guiding her through and then down a hallway where he stopped. He opened a door, giving her a slight push.

"Hurry up. I'm standing right here."

"I'm sorry, but I can't do this with my hands tied," Caution said. "I have to do a number two."

"Oh, for crying out loud!" the man exclaimed. He pulled his knife out once more and cut the tape between Caution's wrists. This allowed her to separate her hands. She put them up in front of her as she made her way to a stall. There were high windows with light coming through, but she didn't think there were any lights on in the bathroom.

"Don't take all day, now," the man said, "and don't do anything stupid. I'll check."

Caution made it into the stall and closed the door. Surprisingly, the man didn't say anything when she locked it. She made her way to the toilet and even found there was toilet paper available. She really did have to go anyway.

"You're not looking, are you? she asked.

"No. I'm not looking," the man said from the doorway, giving a little laugh.

Caution took a chance and lifted the hood slightly to see

what she might. It was a bathroom like so many. Nothing stood out except a big bay of windows at the top of a far wall. The sun was shining, but it was now below the tall windows. Caution believed it was going down with only about an hour of daylight left.

She could hear and see a big airplane not far off and it looked like it was getting ready to land in just a few minutes.

"Are you done, yet?"

"Yes, sir, I'll be right out." Caution pulled the hood down and flushed the toilet. She opened the stall door and walked out.

"Okay, come on," the man said.

"Wait," Caution said, "I have to wash my hands. Don't you wash your hands after going to the bathroom?"

"I'm careful," the man said.

Caution, her hands out in front of her, made her way to the sinks and turned on the water, washing her hands and then getting a handful of water to drink under the hood.

"Don't drink too much," the man warned her, "you'll just have to go to the bathroom again soon and we may not be able to let you go."

The man pulled a couple of paper towels from a dispenser and put them into her hands. She dried her hands and he took the towels as they exited the bathroom, taking her down the corridor and through the door into the space where the box was located. He started looking around and then said some bad words.

"The idiots got the tape in the van, of course. Okay, little princess, back into the box you go."

"But I'd much rather stay out here with you, you're nice," Caution said only to get on his good side.

"You're nice too and very polite, but I have to put you in the box for now or I'll get into a lot of trouble. How about I keep the top open? As long as you behave, of course."

"Okay, I will. Maybe we can play a game." Caution knew exactly what she was doing. This man hurt her Molly. She might be only ten, but she was much wiser than her years.

CHAPTER 7

They were lucky so far; no big rains and the searing heat stayed at bay for now, but they knew it was coming. They made the miles while they could. Only a few wagons were forced to turn around.

A little girl, Mary Swaney, was in such a wagon having contracted cholera. She was in bad shape and it wasn't certain if she would live or not. The wagon was forced to take up a position far in the rear of the wagon train and camp outside the circled wagons. The next day, it headed back hoping to find a doctor at one of the towns or outposts before it was too late.

In another was a man who was accidentally run over by his team and sustained a badly broken leg. If not properly treated soon, it may cause him to become lame or the leg needing to be amputated. His loud moans as the wagon drove off were heard far too long.

There were no other sightings of Indians. However, that didn't mean they weren't there. Hunting parties were not allowed to go out of sight of the wagons and guards were still doubled for the time being. Fires were kept low and weapons were kept loaded and close. A few heads of cattle came up missing, but it wasn't clear if they wandered off or Indians took them. If that was their only loss, they would be lucky.

After a few days of no sightings and no cattle missing, everyone seemed to feel better. The night guards didn't see anything, and hunting parties didn't find any tracks.

The wagon train stopped for two days to rest the animals and do needed repairs and maintenance on the wagons. There was some nice grass with water nearby. They traveled over three-hundred miles. It wouldn't be long, maybe two or three weeks before they would first see the formations called Courthouse Rock and Jailhouse Rock along the way and soon after, come to Chimney Rock. It would mark five-hundred and fifty miles traveled from Independence.

This was a large rock column where wind and rain eroded the rock around it to leave a spire pointing to the sky. It must have been around five-hundred feet tall. The Indians used a name for it which translated into something like 'elk penis'.

It was said you could see it for many miles before getting to it. It was a popular stopping place. It made the travelers happy to see such a landmark. It gave them hope and encouragement to keep going after enduring such a rugged journey. Every day, they would be getting closer to where they were going.

Patrick and Mike got their turn again as night guards. The wagon master tried to split them up, not wanting two people from the same wagon to not get their rest for the next day. However, Patrick and Mike insisted, wanting to share the company of the other. They were getting very close, finding they shared a lot in common, and Mike still felt he owed Patrick more than he could ever repay. He wasn't about to let him do anything dangerous without him.

The night was cool, but not cold. The sky was clear, and the stars glimmered brightly. While keeping an eye out for Indians, Patrick pointed out to Mike the different constellations telling him the stories told to him by his brother. There were even several planets visible with more stories of wild and unbelievable landscapes and the strange creatures roaming across the faraway worlds. Some were believed to be inhabited by beautiful women who kidnapped men from other worlds.

Their time on watch went by quickly and uneventful. On the way back to their wagon, Mike saw a campfire out of its stone circled pit and creeping within just a few inches of a sleeping girl and a few feet from her families wagon. Mike went to put the fire out by stomping on it while Patrick roused the unsuspecting, sleeping family.

The fire set the grass ablaze and singed the blanket but working together they were able to get the fire out before it engulphed the entire blanket of the young girl. No one was hurt, and the family was very grateful. The father, who spoke reasonably good English introduced the family as the Burgmann's, and the mother, not so fluent with the language, insisted Patrick and Mike come by for dinner the following night.

The young girl was maybe sixteen and seemed to be keeping an interested eye on Mike, smiling. The father noticing this would say something to the mother in German and the mother would swat at him and look at her daughter and then Mike. She also smiled.

As Patrick and Mike headed back to their wagon, Patrick mentioned the looks the girl was giving Mike. "You might want to be careful or you might end up taking a bride with you to California," Patrick ribbed him.

"Ain't going to be bloody happenin' anytime this side of the man in the moon," Mike said.

"Well, it looks like there's a glimmer of hope in her parent's eyes and they may be thinking a big son-in-law will give them some good stock in grandkids."

"I'm thinking that be enough talk about such things unless you want to go to bed with a bloody nose," Mike said.

"I'm just telling you what I saw," Patrick stated, putting his hands up. "I would be very careful and keep a good distance from her. Did you even get her name?"

"She said her name was Gertrude," Mike said, puzzled. "What kind of name would that be?"

"It's German, of course," Patrick told him.

"Of course, it's German, you eejit. What self-respecting mother would name her child, Gertrude?"

"A German one?" Patrick guessed, giving a little chuckle.

"It sounds like a sudden sneeze."

"Well, how does Mrs. Gertrude O'Brien sound?"

Mike chased Patrick back to their wagon.

William N. Gilmore

CHAPTER 8

Roger's partner parked the van near the rear of the fast-food joint and went in to use the restroom and order some burgers for all of them. He didn't know what the kid liked, and he really didn't care. Roger's was easy, and he even remembered to order his large diet soda.

He was having trouble getting into his pocket with his bad arm tightly bandaged, making several attempts at getting all the money to pay the bill. After paying, he took the sacks of food and drinks out to the van, again having trouble with his hands full and trying to open the passenger door.

He dropped one of the sacks containing his drink, one for the girl, and Roger's diet soda, causing them to break and spill all the contents. He cursed the ruined sodas as he finally got the door open and placed the remaining sacks on the passenger seat, abandoning the mess sitting in the parking lot. He continued to curse as he went around and got in the driver's seat.

He put the key in the ignition and turned it; nothing. He cursed the stupid ignition. He tried turning the key several more times, jiggling it, checking the lever to make sure it was in park, nothing helped.

After cursing the van this time, he pulled the lever

releasing the hood latch cursing the pain it caused in his damaged arm. He got out and opened the hood fully, hoping it was just a loose battery cable. What he saw confused him. He looked around and then stared back at the engine compartment. The battery cables were not just loose, they were disconnected and somehow, tied in a knot. So were several other wires going to other components of the engine.

"What the...okay, who did this?" he yelled out, looking around at nothing but cars in the parking lot and drive-through. He didn't see anyone in the area who might have done this. Then he panicked a bit, afraid cops may have done it to keep him from driving off. He looked around again, darting his eyes to every vehicle and hunching down a bit, trying to look inconspicuous.

After a few minutes with no cops coming out from under vehicles, behind signs, or dropping out of trees, he relaxed a bit, yet, there was still the van which wouldn't start and no way to fix it. He got out his phone and dialed Roger. He nervously twisted his mustache while holding the phone with the hand of his bad arm. He cursed while waiting for him to answer.

*

Vickie was sitting with Mrs. Murphy while Bill went over to speak with Sean Murphy.

"I hope I didn't start all this," Bill said. "If so, I wish we never found that coin."

"No. If anyone is to blame, it's me. The secret of the

treasure, my obsession with my family's involvement, the history it could change. I've spent a good portion of my life trying to get to the truth of it all, but nothing's worth losing Caution. I'll give them whatever they want."

"What do you think they want?" Bill asked, seeing the pain on Sean's face. Knowing only his daughter's safety mattered now.

"The treasure, of course. Somehow, they know. I mean, I have a good idea where the ship went down and where to find it, but it's not a certainty. I can give them all my research, my maps, my coin, even the journals, just as long as we get Caution back. She's the real treasure.

"It makes no sense," Bill said. "They might get the information, but they'll never be able to go after it. They'll be wanted wherever they go. They can't conduct a big operation like it would take in the open. Police, FBI, every law enforcement agency in the country will be after them."

"I know, and it scares me. How far will they go? What will they do with Caution? She must be so scared." Sean put his hands over his eyes, a soft sob escaped.

The phone rang, startling everyone. Mrs. Murphy jumped up. The FBI team having set up all recording and tracing equipment and giving instructions to Sean to try and keep them talking as long as possible, were ready and gave Special Agent McGill the nod.

Tommy told Sean to answer.

"This is Sean Murphy," he said nervously, his wife holding onto his arm tightly.

An electronically distorted voice began, obviously a recording.

"I know you have the FBI and police there, so I will make this short, Mr. Murphy. Caution is alive and doing well. This will continue as long as you cooperate. Very simply, find the treasure, Mr. Murphy. Find it and then we'll talk some more about your daughter coming home. You will be sent proof of life. Fail, and you will be sent your daughter in a box. You have thirty days." The phone went dead.

"Wait!" Sean yelled into the phone at the disembodied voice, but it wouldn't have done any good anyway.

One of the FBI agents sitting at a control box and wearing headphones looked over at Tommy McGill and shook his head.

Tommy walked over to Mr. Murphy and took the phone from his quivering hand, placing it back on its base.

Mrs. Murphy began to sob, burying her head into her husband's shoulder as he put his arm around her.

"We *will* get her back," Tommy stated with assurance.

Mr. Murphy, barely holding on himself, could only nod his head as he held his crying wife.

Vickey wiped away a few tears as well. Right now,

Caution's safety was her biggest concern, but the call had her boiling and she was beyond angry. Whoever these guys were, no matter what the FBI was going to do, she swore to herself she was going to be the one to get them. She gave Bill a determined look and walked over to the Murphy's. Mr. Murphy raised his head slightly. Looking him straight in the eyes, and giving a nod, she said without any further hesitation, "I'm in."

William N. Gilmore

CHAPTER 9

After a day of feeding the animals, maintenance on the wagon, and cleaning their weapons, Patrick found some quiet time to rest and write in his journal. He put as much detail in it as he could. What they saw, the talk around the camp, even the moods of the different groups as they got further along the trail. Soon, the wagon train would split with some going to Oregon and other destinations while many continued to California.

Patrick and Mike cleaned themselves up for their dinner invitation that evening. However, it didn't go without a little ribbing of Mike from Patrick about the young Burgmann girl.

"You know, it would be nice to have a woman cooking and cleaning for us while we're mining for gold," Patrick stated.

"And just where might you find such a woman who will put up with your bloody wit?" Mike returned.

"Me?" Patrick asked. "I thought you would do the honor of taking a bride."

"I'm not looking to take no bride until I'm old and rich and maybe not even when I'm old. It be the single life for me. I don't need no woman to boss me around and be underfoot all the time. I've got you for that," Mike said with a laugh.

"And what about those cold nights in your castle

overlooking the ocean. Wouldn't you want a woman to snuggle and keep you warm?"

"That's why God made dogs and thick blankets," Mike said. "Neither talk too much and one will obey your commands."

"Who? The dog?" Patrick asked, confused.

"No. The blanket. You tell it to lay down and stay and it won't move all day. Just you bloody try and tell a dog or a woman that."

Patrick laughed out loud. "So, you do have some experience with women."

"Enough. I prefer dogs, blankets if it be cold." Mike said.

"Well, let's be nice and respectful tonight. There won't be any dogs. At least I hope not. I'm not sure what they're cooking."

Mike gave a soured look as the two began the walk towards the Burgmann's camp.

Dinner consisted of a large pot of rabbit stew with a few potatoes thrown in and hand-picked, wild onions. Mrs. Burgmann made some fresh bread for the meal. Making bread was an almost daily thing unless it rained. A big pot of coffee sat on a flat rock by the fire.

There was talk about California, Indians, the mountains they would soon come upon and have to cross, and a few other topics, all of which Mr. Burgmann understood and once in a while he would speak his language to his wife who smiled and nodded her head. The young Gertrude kept her mouth closed in a silent smile most of the night, but her eyes were very often on Mike. It didn't go unnoticed.

At the end of the main meal, Mrs. Burgmann produced from under a cloth, a baked pie made with dried pumpkin from their stores. She served everyone a piece, somehow making sure Mike got the biggest.

"Gertrude make this," she said, smiling. "She cook good."

Mike smiled and looked over at the young girl who was smiling even bigger. He took several bites of the pie, looked again at the girl, nodding his head. "It's very good. Thank you"

Patrick was having a hard time keeping from making any comments or gestures to embarrass Mike. He just observed and kept a stupid smile on his face. He knew there would be a lot of time to talk with and kid Mike later.

The evening would have to end too soon as they were getting an early start in the morning. Patrick and Mike shook hands with everyone, but when Mike tried to shake Mrs. Burgmann's hand, she gave him a big hug. All the Burgmann's stood together as they waved goodbye to the two. As they waved back, Patrick heard them talking very excitedly in their language. Patrick smiled, seemingly understanding what they were saying.

"Just what are you smiling so bloody big about?" Mike asked.

"I think it's nice to have new friends and someone else to talk with besides listening to your dumb pie hole."

"Yes. It was nice. Even if I didn't understand most of it. And speaking of pie—"

"Yeah, it was pretty bad, wasn't it?"

"It took everything in me power not to gag. I didn't want to embarrass the lass, disappoint her. I'm sure she tried her bloody best. She'll get better with time."

"That's all we have out here right now; time. It's going to be nice of you to let her experiment with your stomach."

Mike groaned at the new thought. "Shoot me, shoot me stone-cold dead, right bloody now," Mike pleaded.

CHAPTER 10

"This is good news," Agent Tommy McGill said. "It gives us time to find her and the men who took her."

"I don't think someone having our daughter is good news, Agent McGill," Mrs. Murphy said unhappily. "She should be right here. Things could happen. They might get tired of keeping her, an accident might happen, who knows what is in the minds of these type of men who would take a little girl."

"But she is alive. They must keep her alive and must show you she is alive, "McGill said. "It's not the bloo,—ah, the best possible scenario right now, I know, but it works to our advantage with what we have. They will make mistakes, leave clues, and we will catch them and get Caution back to you."

"How can you be so sure?" Mrs. Murphy asked through a sob.

"Because we have to. There is no other outcome I will accept. No one will rest, no place not looked into, nowhere they can hide."

"Agent McGill," one of the FBI men called out. "There's a call for you from the field office."

"Excuse me," McGill said. He walked over to one of the tables set up and picked up one of the many phones.

"Detective," Mr. Murphy beckoned Vickie over closer to him. Speaking softly, he said. "Whatever you have to do, whatever you need or what it costs, find her. Bring her home safe. I'm not sure the FBI can do that."

"I will," Vickie said, confidence in her voice.

Agent McGill walked over to the center of the room. "I have some information. Good news. The blood found on the dog did not belong to Caution. Initial testing has it typed to a male with O Positive blood. We may have a DNA match to a suspect soon. We are hoping the DNA is from someone who has been matched and is on a database somewhere, either criminal, government, or military. If we can find a match, we have a lot to go on. It should only take a short time. Fingers crossed."

"How long do we have to wait?" Mr. Murphy asked.

"It shouldn't be long. Meanwhile, I need you to start making the motions of getting things ready for your expedition to find this so-called treasure. We need to appease them for the time being. I'm sure we are being watched, or some kind of surveillance is watching our moves."

"I'm not going anywhere while my daughter is out there, in the hands of some evil person or group. How can I do that?" Mr. Murphy exclaimed.

"Because that's how we keep them calm, hesitant to do anything to Caution. Letting them think they are in charge, keep them focused on you, not us. when in fact, we are directing this show. I don't know anything about treasure hunting, other than what I've seen on the telly. I need you to brief me about it. I need you to get their attention and keep it so we can do our job."

"What if I don't find the treasure within the thirty days they demand? What happens to Caution?" Sean asked.

"You'll find it. One way or another and before we wait thirty days. If we don't have a break that gets Caution back in a reasonable amount of time, we'll make a treasure they will want to trade for."

"Won't that be risky, trying to trick them?"

"That's just a contingency plan. I'm sure we'll have her back before that. We're already on the right track with the DNA recovered. It's a major break.

*

Caution was trying to get the man to play a game with her. A game she would control and maybe help her get some answers.

"I saw a man do this at the fair once," She started. "I bet I can guess how old you are and how much you weigh."

"Do you, now? What makes you the expert?" The man snorted.

"I'm just good at guessing. But you have to give me a little help since I can't see you. I'll have to guess just from your voice. Ten pounds on the weight and three years on the age. Deal?"

"And what do I get if you get it wrong? There's always a prize."

"I don't have anything," Caution said. She tried to think of a prize and then it dawned on her. She reached behind her head and removed a tied piece of ribbon, holding her long hair together. Standing tall and with a wave of her other hand pointing to the ribbon, she announces; "Sir, I have this beautiful, first-place blue ribbon for you to attempt to win. It is priceless and has magical properties. There is none finer in the land."

The man smiles and even gives a little giggle at the rendition. "Oh, such a prize," he quips, keeping the charade going. "I will win this for my fair maiden. Take your best guess, my fair lady."

"Let me write it down so there is no question and no cheating."

"I won't cheat. Okay, but the hood stays on." The man put a pen and paper in her hands. She wrote down some numbers the best she could. She folded the paper and handed it out to him. "Don't open it yet. Now, you tell me your birthday and your weight, and I'll write it down and we'll see how close I got.

The man told his birthday and his weight; she wrote it down.

"Okay, open the paper," she tells him.

"You're not even close. You missed it by seven years," the man laughs. "And you think I weigh *that* much? Ha. You're not as good a guesser as you think. I win."

Caution holds out the blue ribbon. "You have fairly won, sir. The prize is yours."

The man takes the blue ribbon, wraps it around his fingers a few times, feeling the silkiness and then tries to put it back in her hand.

"No, sir. She pulls her hand back. It would not be fair for me to take back your win. It is yours."

The man curls it once again into a tight band and puts it in his pants pocket just as his phone begins to play a tune.

"Hello."

A lot of static.

"Hello," the man says again.

Some garbled words are coming through, but it's not clear enough to have a conversation.

"Quin, is that you? Where are you? Are you on the way back? The food better be hot."

Quin. Caution files the name in her brain as the other man. Roger and Quin. And now, she also has Roger's birthday. She has gotten a lot of information, but she realizes it won't do any good unless she can get it to someone. Now to work on finding out exactly where she is.

*

Tom Dearing was livid. He just received the call; his brother, Adam was dead. He wasn't sure how it happened, he just knew his brother called him and told him he took care of the PI watching the lady cop. "No," he stated after being asked, he didn't kill him, he just ruffed him up a little and put him in the trunk of his own car. He tossed his gun one way and the car keys another. He was going to see what she and her boyfriend knew, maybe have a little fun with her.

Tom Dearing told him he didn't think that was such a good idea. She was a real detective after all, not one of those fake cops. If he did, he better not leave a witness or any evidence.

Adam Dearing agreed. He was sure the PI never saw his face, but just to be certain, he said after he got through with her and her boyfriend, he'd go back and finish him off.

Now, his brother was dead. How and by whose hand didn't matter right now. The lady cop and the PI were alive. "But not for long," Tom Dearing swore under his breath. He made a call to a familiar number, to someone he knew he could trust to get the job done right and who would be eager to take revenge on Adam's killer.

CHAPTER 11

Bill gently took Vickie's arm and guided her outside, away from all the other people crowding around.

"Are you sure this is what you want to do?" Bill asked.

"I need to do this. They're counting on me." Vickie stated.

"It sounds like you're letting your emotions dictate your decision. Take a breath, think clearly, maybe even take some time. It's possible you could be more help while you have a badge and the resources."

"We already went over this. The brass doesn't want me anywhere near this case. You know how they are. I've made up my mind. I thought you were going to support me?"

"I do," Bill said. "I'm just making sure you know what you're getting into. Playing the Devil's advocate, I guess, justifying everything once again in my own head."

"And?" she asked with questioning eyes.

"I'm with you, partner" he smiled. "So, what do you want to do first?"

"It's already late afternoon. Let's go find that private investigator and see what he knows before the FBI screws it up. I want to know why he lied to you, why they were watching us in the first place, and what his connection is with the Dearing's."

"I'll call Lieutenant Cummings and give him the news. I sure figured Olson out wrong. Maybe I've been out of the game too long. Retirement may have caused me to lose some of my edge."

"Your good instinct told you to not give Olson his gun back," Vickie stated. "No telling what might have happened if you did. I don't think you've lost anything."

"There's something I don't understand," Bill said. "If Olson and Dearing are involved together, why was Olson's man attacked, and by whom?"

It was already dark when Bill and Vickie arrived at the Peachtree Street address Mr. Murphy gave them for Olson's firm. It was a well-known, large building with over thirty floors. They checked in the lobby, finding the office suite listed on the building occupant's directory as 1525. They stepped into one of the elegant elevators and Bill pushed the button for the fifteenth floor.

"How do you want to handle this?" Vickie asked. "Good cop-bad cop, or do you just want to beat it out of him?"

Bill chuckled. "Let's just see what he has to say first and play it by ear. He's experienced and not one to fall for any tricks or threats. I just want to get to the truth."

"Alright. I'll follow your lead, but if I sense he was involved with Caution's abduction in any way, we'll get it out of him, one way or another."

The elevator stopped, and the doors opened on the fifteenth floor. An arrow pointed to the left for the odd-numbered suites which included 1525.

Bill and Vickie arrived at the door with a gold-colored plaque to one side of it with the suite number and OLSON INVESTIGATIONS imprinted on it in black.

Bill gave Vickie a look, raising his eyebrows up and down a few times in quick succession and then opened the door. There was an outer office for a receptionist, however, there was no one there. There was a couch, a few chairs, and a table with magazines scattered on it. It looked like any ordinary office waiting area.

They went in, closing the door behind them and went to the desk. There were information forms for potential clients to fill out, and pamphlets with information on the firm and a list of services. A picture of a smiling Olson was on the front. A nameplate on the desk read; Judy Henderson – Executive Assistant.

After several minutes, Bill, already antsy, went to a closed door leading to the rest of the office. He knocked on the door, twice, but got no response either time.

"I don't know if anyone is here," he said. "Maybe they went to lunch."

"Why would they leave the doors unlocked? Try the

door," Vickie said.

Bill checked the door and it opened into a hallway leading to several other offices, their doors also closed.

"Is anyone here?" Bill called out. There was silence.

"I don't like this," Vickie said.

"Neither do I." Bill pulled out his semi-automatic. "Stay behind me."

"Why?" She asked. "You have another gun for me to pull from your back?"

Bill looked back and saw Vickie with her pistol already out. He smiled.

Bill went to the first door. There was a frosted glass top with Gerald Olson's name printed on it. He checked the handle. It opened easily. He pushed the door open and took a quick look. A desk, chair, couch, bookcase, the usual stuff, but no one was there. Vickie kept an eye on his back as he went in and made a check behind the desk just to make sure.

He came out and went across the hall to the next office. D. R. TANNER, was painted on the door glass; the name of Olson's associate, now with a broken nose. It too was unlocked. He pushed the door open and could immediately smell a strong odor of gunpowder in the air.

When Bill looked in, he saw there was someone there. This someone was on the floor with a large bandage over the bridge of his nose and a nice, round hole in his forehead. His sightless eyes staring at the ceiling. Blood splatter was on the far wall and covered several pictures and certificates. Tanner was wearing a shoulder holster with an S&W 9mm still snapped in. His coat hung neatly on a coat rack in the corner.

"He's D. R. T.," Bill said.

"Tanner?" Vickie asked.

"Yep, that's him. D. R. T. is D. R. T.; Dead Right There. Let's see if there's anyone else here before we call this in."

A set of bathrooms were checked, and no one was found, however, Vickie stated there was evidence someone appeared to have recently washed in the women's bathroom. There were small traces of blood in and on the wet sink and as well as a still wet paper towel in the trash.

There was one more door down the hallway. FILE ROOM was on the glass. Bill turned the handle and pushed the door open. It was dark inside. He reached around the door frame to find a light switch without exposing himself too much. His fingers found the switch and Bill flipped it on.

The lights came on with a buzz from the florescent bulbs giving a view of file cabinets, a large copy machine, a big table and chairs, and another door. This one was solid and may have been to a supply room or a broom closet.

Bill directed Vickie to open it as he held his pistol out, pointed at the door. When the door opened, Bill heard a gasp from inside the closet.

"Come out with your hands where I can see them," Bill demanded. "And they better be empty."

"Please don't hurt me," a woman's hysterical voice pleaded. "I didn't see anything. I don't know anything."

"We're with the police," Vickie called into the small room. "It's safe to come out."

There was some movement and a box fell over. Behind another box on the floor, the feet and pant-covered legs of a woman first appeared. They scooted out from behind the box until she was fully out in the open. "Are you really from the police?" She asked, obviously scared and shaken.

"I'm Detective Winston," Vickie stated, stepping towards the woman, and offering her hand to help her get up. "Are you injured?"

Bill, still unsure who the woman was, stood back with his pistol still out. He observed something a little strange on her arm.

"No. Is Mr. Tanner okay?"

"Who are you? What happened here?" Bill asked, not ready to tell her about the body in the other office.

"I'm Judy Henderson. I'm just the office secretary. Mr. Olson just left, and I was getting some files when someone came in and Mr. Tanner began to argue with them. They went into his office and a few minutes later, I heard what I thought was a muffled gunshot. So, I hid here in the closet about twenty minutes ago. Did he call you guys? Is Mr. Tanner alright? He's not hurt, is he?"

"You're safe now, Judy," Vickie said, putting her arm around her. "Did you see anyone? Do you know who it was who came in?"

"No. Why won't you tell me about Mr. Tanner? Is he...is he hurt?"

"He's been shot," Vickie told her finally. "He didn't make it."

The woman crumbled into Vickie's arms and went to the floor in a heap. It was all Vickie could do to keep from dropping her. She fainted and was out for the count.

They made her as comfortable as possible on a couch in the waiting room and called for an ambulance and back-up units.

"Who do you think did this, Dearing?" Vickie asked.

"Maybe."

"Why? And where's Olson? How's he mixed up in all of this?"

"A bunch of good questions," Bill stated. "I wish I could answer just one of them. I have a few more to add myself."

Lieutenant Cummings came into the private investigator's office and found Bill and Vickie standing over a woman on a couch.

"Who'd you shoot this time?" he asked, removing his fedora and shaking his head.

"We didn't shoot anyone," Bill said. "We found him like

that."

"Him?" the Lieutenant questioned, looking at the woman.

"Tanner, one of the P.I.'s here, back in his office," Bill said. "This is Judy Henderson, she works here too. She didn't see much, but may have heard the intruder. She fainted."

"What are you even doing here? You're retired. You're not even in the reserves. You're creating a conflict. And you," he pointed at Vickie, "You're skating on thin ice. Captain Pealor won't be happy. Not even a little bit. You're supposed to be a Burglary Detective and here you are, involved not with just one but two deaths in two days. At least one of them shot by you."

"But in self-defense," Bill added. "And she saved my sorry butt too."

Lieutenant Cummings gave Bill a distasteful look.

"We're trying to find a scared little girl before something else bad happens to her," Vickie blurted out.

"You're talking about the Murphy girl. That's an FBI case. What's Olson or the dead guy got to do with her kidnapping? What are you not telling me, Winston? You'd better come clean before this gets you in any deeper."

When the EMT's arrived, they assisted Mrs. Henderson by using ammonia carbonate capsules to bring her around. They placed her on a gurney for transport to Grady Hospital to be checked out just to be safe.

CHAPTER 12

The wagon wheels kept on turning no matter what happened on the trail. It was the wagon master's duty to get the wagons across the plains in the quickest time possible. If a wagon broke down, it was the owner's responsibility to fix it or leave it behind, but if it blocked a path and was delaying the rest, it was moved for them, sometimes being tipped over or pushed off a cliff if need be.

One night, during a security patrol, a man accidentally shot himself in the foot when he laid his loaded and capped rifle up against a wagon and it fell over and discharged. The ball took a couple of toes off and he ended up having to ride the rest of the way while making his wife walk alone beside the wagon.

A young boy not paying attention or who fell asleep while walking too close to his wagon got run over. The family of five was devastated but only stopped for an hour to bury him, not wanting to fall too far behind and becoming a target for Indians.

These types of accidents were common along the many trails as were the dreadful diseases which plagued virtually every wagon train heading west. More people died from those afflictions than were killed by Indians and accidents combined. Their graves marked by rocks or simple wooden slats.

In truth, most Indians only wanted to trade or beg for food, a bit of clothing, or maybe some liquor. Many were worse off than the poor immigrants crossing the plains. Sometimes though, they resolved to steal horses or cattle and sometimes they banded into small raiding parties. Most of those were young braves armed with only their bows and arrows, tomahawks, knives, war clubs, or lances. Few carried firearms.

A popular rite of passage with the young braves was to taunt each other into getting close enough to an enemy to touch or strike them with a stick, spear, tomahawk, or some other instrument without injuring them or getting injured. Sometimes it was to get close enough to steal something belonging to the enemy. It was something to show their bravery to the others. The stick or spear would be adorned with notches or feathers which may have been given as an award for their bravery. Lavish stories would be told by the brave himself about his bravery and showing off his decorated stick or other items. The French in the 1870s gave this instrument the name of 'coup stick' and the tally of touches would be referred to as 'counting coup'.

With some Indians, it wasn't feathers or notches marking their triumphs, it was scalps. The more they collected on their spears and lances, or hanging from their lodges, the braver they were and sometimes the higher position within the tribe.

But some white men also took trophies. They would wear necklaces of ears cut from the Indians they killed and sometimes they also collected scalps, trading them for goods with sutlers or at forts much like beaver pelts.

Many men of all races were seen with shaven heads, not wanting to be a target for the Indians and to show they were not worthy of being killed. Women kept their hair in a bun or covered by a scarf.

Mike wasn't about to get his head shaved and kept his hat over his thick hair most of the time. Besides, it provided cover from the sun and the dust of the trail, not to mention, he thought it made him look older and more like an American than an Irishman.

After several more weeks on the trail, the large formations of Jailhouse Rock and Courthouse Rock came into view. At first, approaching from the east, the rock structures looked like a single enormous structure rising out of the plateau, but as you got closer, you could see they were two separate formations.

Coming within less than ten miles of them, many were tempted to travel the distance to get a closer look and even attempt to scale the monuments, however, the wagon master made no plans to take any detour which would delay them at least a day or more from their route.

Instead, off in the distance, maybe twenty or more miles, they could just see the top of the famous Chimney Rock and they would be stopping there in two or three days. There would be a good camping area with a good stream and they could spend a full day or two there.

Many people climbed Chimney Rock and quite a few wrote their names in the clay, sandstone, and volcanic ash making up the mound and spire, once having been over five-hundred feet or more in elevation. The pioneers were fortunate to have a once-in-a-lifetime chance to see all three of the magnificent creations of nature and to have the stories to tell.

Patrick, in awe of their wonder and beauty, wrote about them in his journal and even drew pictures of the monuments. He couldn't wait to get to Chimney Rock and put his own name there for others following behind to know who came before them. He was a true trailblazer.

He was glad there was something else to look at besides the nasty back end of an ox and clouds of dust. Even if he took Midnight for a ride or went with a hunting party, there was little change in scenery. Or in color.

The same routine, day after day, week after week, got tiring on the mind as well as the body. Sometimes he wished for some Indians to show up just to give a little excitement. The most stimulating thing to happen lately was a meteor shower one night which put on quite a show. Mike even talked about going over to see Gertrude, so he knew he was feeling it too.

Chimney Rock, near the Platte River, took up a lot of the ongoing conversations with lots of excitement and anticipation.

Not too long after Chimney Rock, they would come to Fort Laramie. There they would have a chance to get fresh supplies, if they were still stocked and not wiped out by a previous wagon train, hear some news even if it was six months old, and see a lot of different people. They might even add a few wagons to their troupe.

Sometimes they would come across wagons and riders heading east. Some who hauled freight back and forth and some who gave up on the dream of getting rich or who just wanted to get back to loved ones left behind.

They hoped there would be good news for the trail ahead and there were promising reports back from the goldfields of California.

CHAPTER 13

Caution sat in the open box, the hood still over her head, not knowing how to get the information to find out where she was and if she did, how to get the information to someone so they could find her. She desperately wanted to get back to her parents and find out about Molly.

"I'm really hungry," Caution stated without it sounding like she was whining. "Did you say your friend is bringing some food?"

"Yeah. He'll be back in a few minutes. He's getting some burgers. You like burgers?"

"Sometimes," Caution responded. "My mother doesn't like me to eat fast food. She says it's not good for you. Too much fat and calories."

"That's what makes it taste so good," Roger said, giving a snicker. "I bet you go out to fancy restaurants with your folks all the time and eat steak, lamb, and lobster. You get those big desserts."

"No. My mom is a great cook. Sometimes I help. Once in a while, we get something delivered, but not often. My father works a lot and sometimes gets home late."

"Yeah, he works in his big, fancy building downtown

with his name on it. He's rich. Why's he work?"

"We're not rich," Caution said, trying not to lose her temper. "My dad works hard every day. How do you know where he works?"

"That's for me to know and for you to find out, little miss."

Just then, Roger's phone rang the funny tune again. He turned to Caution. "Not a word, young lady." Roger answered, "Yeah?"

"Roger, it's Quin. Something funny is going on."

"What are you talking about, don't they have any diet drinks?"

"Not that, you idiot. It's the van. It won't start. Somehow the wires got...well, twisted."

"Twisted? I don't understand. Did you run over something?"

"No. I'm at the burger place. I parked and went inside, got the food, and came out and it wouldn't start. I looked under the hood and the battery wires are in a knot. I can't get them loose. And they're not the only ones. I think someone did it as a joke, but there's no one here. What should I do?"

Roger thought for a moment. "You can't leave it there like that and you can't get it towed. You'll need to clean it out, wipe it down. Get all the fingerprints off and make sure there's nothing that can be traced back to us. It was rented under a false name and ID, so if you do your job, it won't matter."

"Won't matter? How do I get back to the warehouse?"

"You walk. You're only a mile or so up the road. It won't take you long."

"Don't expect the burgers to be warm when I get there, and you can forget about me carrying any drinks for a mile with my arm torn up."

"Just get here as quick as you can. Don't miss anything on the van, including under the hood. And bring back the tool bag. We'll need the tape, and some of the other stuff."

"This ain't my first rodeo," Quin said. He hung up and went back inside the restaurant and to the restroom getting a bunch of paper towels and a large cup of water. He added a little of the liquid hand soap for good measure.

He started on the hood and wiped it down to include the inside just as Roger told him. He would have forgotten otherwise.

He got in and wiped it clean on the inside, including the hood release. Something even Roger forgot to tell him. His arm was killing him, but he needed to get it done. After about thirty minutes of wiping in and out, he threw away several large wads of towels, grabbed the bag of now cold burgers and the tool bag and started the walk to the warehouse.

*

"It looks like it will be a little longer before we get those burgers," Roger said.

"Okay," Caution said, rocking with her knees up to her chin with her arms around them, her mind on something else.

A mile from the burger place. Caution overheard Roger's side of the conversation and put another bit of information along with the rest she was gathering. But there was something else she was thinking about as well. *How did Roger know where father worked? Was it possible he could have been there before? Maybe on the night father was mugged?*

CHAPTER 14

There was no getting out of it this time. Bill and Vickie needed to tell Lieutenant Cummings just enough of the information about their involvement with the Murphy's to put the story together. Vickie even told him about her decision to put in for retirement and work for the Murphy's.

"That's a lot to download," the lieutenant stated. "Have you told anyone else in the department about your decision?"

"No," Vickie said. "I just made up my mind today."

"Don't."

"Don't tell or don't retire?" Vickie asked, confused.

"I wish I could say don't retire, you're too good of a cop to lose, but that's up to you. I wouldn't tell anyone you're going to be working for the Murphy's. Not yet. With the young girl still missing, and it being an FBI case, you may not want to give up your resources just yet. A lot of the guys who retire go into business for themselves; P.I.'s, protective services, skip chasers, and the like. But they keep their contacts and get help and favors from the ones still here. You know, like record checks, pictures, fingerprint checks, mainly small stuff, but things which could get them in trouble. So, sometimes they throw them a little extra cash once in a while. Going to work for a millionaire family just sours the notes a bit, if you catch my drift."

"Okay, put in my papers and keep quiet about the job. Got you," Vickie said.

"Now, if you two don't mind, I still need statements from you. You don't need to go into all the explanation, I just need something to put it all together in a nice, neat little package for the captain."

Almost two hours later at police headquarters, Bill and Vickie finished their statements for the homicide detectives on the case. Just before leaving, they learned Judy Henderson left the hospital as soon as she got there without checking in, making a statement, providing any information, or notifying the homicide office.

The sun was just going down as they walked to Bill's car in the visitor's lot.

"We still need to find Olson," Vickie said.

"It would help. We might get a few more answers," Bill agreed.

"What now?" Vickie asked as they reached the car and were getting in.

Once they were buckled in, Bill turned to Vickie and asked, "Have you ever done any night fishing?"

Vickie blinked a few times and shaking her head with a questionable look stated, "Not since I was a little girl with my father. Why?"

"I just have a feeling they may be biting tonight. We might just get lucky."

"Tonight? With Caution missing and dressed like this?" Vickie asked, bewildered. "Besides, all my fishing equipment is in storage."

"Gear," Bill laughed. "It's fishing gear. You've got everything you'll need with you; you'll see." Bill pulled out of the lot heading downtown.

"You're a strange one for sure, Bill Warner," Vickie said.

Several minutes later, Bill pulled into the parking garage across the street from the building where the Olson Investigations' office was located.

"Why are we back here?" Vickie asked.

"Hopefully to catch a big one," Bill said. He reached into the center seat console and took something out, placing it in his inside coat pocket. "Let's go. I hope we're not too late or that we didn't spook our prey."

They left the garage, walking across Peachtree Street to the large building. The main doors were still open, and they took an elevator to the fifteenth floor.

The main door to Olson Investigations was blocked with two bands of yellow crime scene tape in an 'X', secured with only clear plastic tape. Bill unpeeled the sticky tape on one side of the door. He checked the door and found it was now locked.

"I thought it would be," he said.

"Now what? Vickie questioned.

"That's why I brought these," Bill said, reaching into his coat and bringing out a small black case. Opening it, Bill showed her a set of lock picks. "I've been practicing.

"You've got to be kidding me?" Vickie blurted out. "You have the right to remain silent," Vickie started.

Bill laughed removing two of the small instruments. One was a rake pick, the other a tension bar. "They seldom get this right on TV. You see guys opening doors with only one pick. It doesn't work that way."

"You do realize you're talking to a burglary detective, right?"

"I think I'll just remain silent," Bill said.

"Good idea," Vickie laughed.

It took Bill another few minutes of grunting and twisting his mouth just right to get the lock opened and they went into the office. The lights were left on. Bill secured the crime scene tape once again, closing the door and locking it.

"Keep an eye on the door," he whispered to Vickie. "Come get me if anyone tries to come in. I'm going fishing."

"Good luck," Vickie whispered back.

"Thanks." Bill headed for the file room.

About ten minutes later, Vickie saw the silhouette of someone at the main office door. She held her breath and her eyes got big. She placed her hand on her weapon. The person stood there for a second, then walked off. Slowly, Vickie let the air out and relaxed a bit. She wished Bill would hurry.

A few minutes later, he came out of the file room, closing the door behind him and holding a large manila envelope with something sticking out of it.

"We caught a shark," he whispered with a big smile.

Just then, they heard someone working on the lock at the office door. They quickly and silently retreated to Olson's office and went in, barely closing the door behind them, going flat against the wall next to the door. They both took out their weapons.

The person got the office door open, much quicker than Bill did, closing it behind them. They could hear the footsteps as the person got to and opened the file room door; opened it but didn't close it.

Bill and Vickie opened the door to Olson's office and moved to the now open file room door. Bill reached in and flipped the switch turning on the room's lights. There was a quick movement in the supply closet.

"Come on out. I have what you are looking for Ms. Henderson, or whatever your name is," Bill demanded.

Judy Henderson walked out of the closet. "Oh, hi detectives. I thought I lost my wallet in the closet while hiding there and was trying to locate it. Did one of the officers happen to find it?"

"Don't even try that with us," Bill said. "I have what you were looking for. The gun you shot Tanner with." He held up the envelope containing a Ruger .22 semi-automatic with a silencer attached.

"I don't know what you're talking about," she started. "Why would I shoot my boss? I told you and the other detectives what happened." Her eyes were looking around and at the doorway, calculating.

"You won't make it," Bill said. "Sit down over there, now, and sit on your hands," he said, indicating the couch, not moving the pistol he pointed at her.

She gave Bill a sneer and grudgingly went over to the couch and sat down without saying anything else.

"Call Lieutenant Cummings," he told Vickie. "We caught us a barracuda."

Within fifteen minutes, the office was swarming again with detectives and patrolmen. Henderson was now in handcuffs. Lieutenant Cummings came in, shaking his head.

"At least you didn't shoot her," he said.

"If I hadn't found this in time, I might have been forced to," Bill said, turning the envelope containing the handgun over to the lieutenant. "She hid it in the back of the closet in a box of stationery.

"How did you know?"

"It was the totality of little things adding up. The

gunpowder odor was still strong although she said she heard the muffled shot twenty minutes before we arrived. Tanner was apparently killed by someone he knew, trusted, or didn't consider a threat. He never got his gun out. There were some pinpoint spots of blood on the woman's arm. Blowback from the gunshot, I believe, and then there was some blood on the sink and a wet paper towel in the *women's* restroom. She called herself just a secretary. Someone who was an executive assistant would not call herself just a secretary. She fainted and was taken to the hospital but left without being seen or notifying anyone. No weapon was found, so I believed she would come back to retrieve it. I found it first."

"You want to come back and work homicide for me?" The lieutenant asked.

"Not in this lifetime," Bill said. "The only thing I want is to have a chance for Vickie and me to question her at your office."

"I don't know about that."

"We caught your killer for you, you owe us."

"The captain will have my hide."

"Give us just ten minutes. It's important," Vickie pleaded.

"Is this about the little Murphy girl too?"

"We don't know yet. We need to find out," she said.

Looking Bill's way, "You're still a civilian," he told him.

"I might get away with it if it's just Vickie."

"Fine. Let's just get it done," Bill said. "Time's not on our side."

The lieutenant nodded.

Bill and Vickie returned to the Atlanta Police Headquarters and went to the offices of the Homicide Squad. Bill was taken into the observation room where Lieutenant Cummings was waiting.

A large, two-way mirror allowed them to see the woman who claimed to be Judy Henderson sitting at a table facing them without themselves being seen. A digital-video-recording-camera was set up in the observation room and they turned the audio on as well.

She was handcuffed by both wrists to a bar on the top of the metal table. They saw Vickie come in, file folder in hand, and sit at one end of the table.

The first thing Vickie did was introduce herself again and then put a paper in front of her and then read the woman her Miranda warnings from another sheet of paper. There was just enough room with her hands cuffed for the woman to sign the paper, acknowledging her rights were read to her, when Vickie handed her a pen.

Vickie took the pen back and looked at the signature placing it into the file folder in front of her.

"What is your name, your real name?"

"Toni Mason.

"Where is the real Judy Henderson?" Vickie asked.

"I understand she's on maternity leave," the woman said.

"Where is Gerald Olson?"

"I have no idea."

"Why did you shoot Tanner?"

"I never said I shot him."

"Yeah, right. What do you know about the kidnapping of Caution Murphy?"

"Who? I don't know anything about a kidnapping."

"Is Olson involved with her kidnapping?"

"Look. I told you I don't know about any kidnapping."

"A little ten-year-old girl was taken from the Murphy home earlier today by at least two men. If you know anything about it, it could go a long way with the District Attorney."

"Again, I don't know anything. We're done. I want my attorney. I'm not saying another word."

Vickie picked up the folder and left the interrogation room. She walked around to the observation room where Bill and the lieutenant were waiting.

"Well, that was a bust," Lieutenant Cummings said. "I think you pushed her too far on the kidnapping until she lawyered up. Now we can't question her about the murder. I knew this was a mistake."

"Not really," Vickie said. "We have what might be her

real name. We need to check her fingerprints and get her record. I'm sure she has one. Also, if we can find the address, you might want to get someone over to the real Judy Henderson's residence and check on her. I'd put a BOLO out for Olson."

"She's no rookie," Bill said to the lieutenant. "She wasn't going to answer any questions or give any information about anything else."

"We'll never know now, will we?" The lieutenant said.

CHAPTER 15

They were five-hundred and fifty miles from Independence, MO. They braved the trail now for about eight weeks. Starting with almost a hundred wagons, they were down to about ninety. Unfortunately, they also buried several people along the way; family, friends, not one a stranger.

Chimney Rock was a magnificent sight. It gave some people hope as well as a sense of accomplishment. Patrick declared it should be added as one of the natural wonders of the world. He needed to crane his neck back till it hurt and cover his eyes when he looked towards the top of its tall, center spire. It rose to nearly five-hundred feet high. There was so much rubble around its base, he believed it may have reached six or seven hundred feet or maybe even a thousand feet at one time.

Several people dared to climb as high as they could to add their names with so many others on the rock. Mike and Patrick were satisfied to just write on some of the rocks at the base.

The wagon train was going to stay for at least two days to rest the animals where there was good water and grass. Fort Laramie, a newly established military outpost with sutlers, blacksmiths, a hospital, and even a bakery was less than a week away and they were hoping the last wagon train hadn't wiped out all the supplies. Wagons could get repaired there. Tired, starving, or injured animals could be exchanged for fresh, for a price.

You needed to make sure you were supplied and ready for the long push west. Once the wagons got on the other side of the Continental Divide, things became much more difficult.

The Continental Divide, also referred to as the Great Divide, discovered by the Meriwether Lewis and William Clark Expedition, also known as the Corps of Discovery, was where all the watersheds on the east of the divide would drain to the Atlantic Ocean and all the watersheds on the west of the divide would drain to the Pacific Ocean. It did not divide the county in the middle as the name might be misinterpreted.

With light from the campfire, Patrick wrote in his journal as he listened to the coyotes howling and Mike snoring. Many other campfires dotted the interior of the circled wagons. People were talking and singing, some even dancing around their fires to various musical instruments; squeezeboxes, harmonicas, jaw harps, and others made from whatever would make a sound, children running and laughing, some men arguing over anything and everything, and even a few dogs barking.

Patrick and Mike wouldn't have to go on security watch for another several days. Their supply of food and water was adequate. Their oxen and Midnight were in pretty good shape; well-fed, and watered. Hunting and fishing were successful, and the meat shared around.

There also wasn't a reported case of cholera in the wagon train for several weeks. Life was good for the time being. Enjoy the rest, take care of the animals, see some of the sights. There was a lot of trail behind them and even more ahead of them. With every mile the dangers also seemed to escalate. Tomorrow was promised to no man.

CHAPTER 16

There was a knock at the door of the warehouse. Roger looked out and saw it was Quin. He opened the main door next to the roll-up and Quin lumbered in.

"It's still hot as blazes out there," he said. His shirt was stained in several places from sweat and what little hair he still possessed was hanging down on his forehead, damp and stringy. He tossed a paper bag at Roger.

"It's not hot tonight, you're just out of shape," Roger said. His first try in closing the door failed as it must have stuck on something. He gave it a nudge with his shoulder and got it closed and locked.

Quin looked over and saw the box with Caution's hooded head sticking out of the top. "Why is the top not on?"

"She needed to go to the bathroom," Roger said. "She's been good. The hood never came off. You have the bag with the tape."

"Has there been any word, yet?" Quin put the tool bag down.

"No. I haven't heard anything." Roger opened the paper bag and took one of the wrapped hamburgers, walked over to Caution and put it in her hands.

"You untied her too?" Quin asked.

"I told you I took her to the bathroom."

"Oh, okay, I understand. Why didn't you tie her back up when she was done?"

"Someone took the tape with them," shaking his head and making a stupid face at Quin.

"Well, I didn't know you were going to untie her, and I was planning on coming right back."

"You wiped the van all down, right?" Roger questioned him.

"Yes, I wiped it down, all of it, including under the hood and even the hood release."

"The hood release?"

"Yeah, I didn't think you'd think of that. It put my prints on the pull latch when I pulled it to release the hood. See. I'm not so dumb."

"Very smart. You do the mirrors too?"

"I did it all. It's clean as a whistle, now eat your stupid hamburger," Quin insisted.

Caution took off the paper around the burger. The name of the fast-food burger place, 'Jim's Juicy Burgers', on the wrapper. She ate the cold burger without anything to drink and folded the wrapper, putting it in her pocket. It was one of the most satisfying hamburgers she ever ate.

*

"Now that just pisses me off," the manager of Jim's Juicy Burgers said to his employee while they were on a cigarette break. "I saw this guy drop his bag of sodas and he just left them on the ground. He didn't bother throwing the trash away. And then he starts washing his van in the parking lot, using our supplies no less, and now he just leaves it sitting in the parking lot while he's off into the night to who knows where doing who knows what. What a jerk."

The manager walked over to the van and looked in. No one was there. Then he went to the back of the van and pounded on the back doors.

There were no windows on the side or in the back. No one opened the doors and he couldn't hear anything as he listened for movement.

"It would serve him right if I were to call the cops and have it towed."

"I think you should," the employee agreed. "That's not right leaving it here. Where do you think he went?"

"Who knows? Who cares? I'm calling the cops."

Fifteen minutes later, a patrol car pulled into the parking lot. The manager came out to talk with the officer and pointed out the white van.

"This guy was washing his van right here in our parking lot, with our towels and then he just left. I don't know if he's coming back or not. It's been several hours. We close in three. I want you to have it towed away."

"I'm sorry," the officer said. "It's on private property, I can't do it. Do you have any signs about towing abandoned vehicles? If so, you can call the wrecker company and have it towed yourself."

"I think there's one in the back. Let me look."

Sure enough, there was a warning sign on one of the light poles behind the restaurant for leaving vehicles unattended for over two hours or they could be towed at the owner's expense. There was a phone number for the wrecker company as well.

"There you go," the officer said. "You've solved your own dilemma and now you'll know for future problems like this."

"Thanks," the manager said as the police car drove away. "Thanks, for nothing." He went inside and called the number that was on the sign. A nice lady said they would send out a driver right away.

The manager went back to the front of the restaurant and told the employees there would be no more free food for the lazy, no-good cops.

The officer drove down the street and pulled over into a shopping center parking lot. He sat there for several minutes watching traffic, waiting for someone to run the red light.

Something was bothering him. There was this invisible finger he sometimes felt, poking him in the forehead, letting him know there was something he forgot or was supposed to do. This time, it was gnawing him with a vengeance.

He forgot to log the call. He picked up his metal notebook and wrote the address and the call times on the patrol log on top of several other papers. He looked up, thinking, trying to remember something else when he saw a wrecker drive by. *It may be on its way to Jim's for that white van,* he thought.

He shook his head and then put the patrol car in drive, getting ready to pull back out onto the roadway when he made a quick stop, throwing the gearshift into park. He picked up his notebook and lifted the log sheet to another piece of paper. There it was. A BOLO on a white van involved in a kidnapping. Two men, no tag, no other information.

He pulled out into the street and hurried back to the restaurant parking lot, his blue lights illuminating the night, pulling in just as the big driver was lowering the flatbed of the wrecker behind the van.

The officer got out of the patrol car and went up to the huge wrecker driver. "I'm going to have to hold your call on this one, my friend. I need to call it in. I think there's a BOLO out on it."

"Ah, shucks," the massive man said. "I'm Bubba Thompson, the new wrecker driver for Mr. Granger. This was going to be my very first solo pick up—*ever*. I hope he's not going to be mad at me. Ah, by the way, what's a BOLO?"

CHAPTER 17

A detective who was assigned the duty to check on her was happy to report the real Judy Henderson was at a hospital giving birth. She was fine, and he left a card with her husband telling him it was just an identity theft case they were investigating and just needed to verify some information when she was up to it.

He didn't mention what happened in her office. The husband was confused she needed to call the Homicide Squad about an identity theft investigation, but for the moment, there were other things on his mind, such as his wife and their little seven-pound daughter who just came into the world.

A check was made of Teri Mason's fingerprints and they matched a different name in the NCIC database. No surprise there.

She was arrested in California on an auto theft charge under the name Theresa Kline. She was seventeen at the time. The arrest also included the additional charges of eluding the police, aggravated assault with a motor vehicle, shoplifting, and about half a dozen traffic violations. The District Attorney charged her as an adult. She was convicted and served two years in a California correctional facility. Records of crimes she may have committed while still a juvenile were unavailable. The records were sealed by court order as was done with most juvenile offenders.

However, it seemed to be more than a coincidence she was from the same area as Dearing, both now in Atlanta, and their paths crossing on this investigation. A deeper look into both was warranted.

Although Winston was not assigned to Homicide, she was allowed to have access to the files on Teri Mason aka Theresa (Terry) Kline and Tom Dearing per order of Captain Pealor. Bill Warner was considered an unpaid civilian consultant and also given access. This was because of their long, honorable service, involvement in the case, and their unique knowledge about the suspects and victims.

Bill asked for the files on Olson and Tanner, knowing they would do a full work-up on anyone remotely connected to the homicide. It would be several hours before they received all the paperwork from the Records Section.

Lieutenant Cummings came into the squad room where Vickie and Bill were going over files.

"We may have caught a break on the Murphy girl's kidnapping," he gave the news. "A patrolman located an abandoned white van in the parking lot of a fast-food restaurant. A man left it there after he was seen washing it down."

He gave Vickie the address and she and Bill wasted no

time getting out of the office.

Fifteen minutes later they pulled into the parking lot of Jim's Juicy Burgers. The lot was full of police cars, detective cars, black SUV's, a tow truck, and a lot of people wearing dark blue jackets with yellow 'FBI' printed on the backs. Light towers were set up around the parking lot.

Special Agent in Charge Tommy McGill and several other agents were talking with a man in the parking lot while an FBI forensic team was going over the van. Orange traffic cones and yellow crime scene tape surrounded it. When he saw Bill and Vickie, McGill left the man with the other agents and walked over to them.

"Is that the one?" Vickie asked before he even got to them.

"We don't bloody know yet," he said, a little miffed at their arrival. "It's a good possibility. We're working on it. Why are you here?"

"To see if we can help. I'd think you'd want all the help you could get on this. All the eyes, ears, and expertise you could muster. We're not talking about a lost puppy here."

"I know what needs to be done, detective. This isn't my first case. I just don't want someone who is overly emotional getting—

"Overly emotional?" Vickie blurted out, causing several people to stop and look their way. "Maybe you need someone overly emotional to remind you what's really at stake here, Agent McGill."

"Believe me, detective, I bloody well know. I will use every resource the FBI has and anything it doesn't to find the little girl and return her unharmed to her parents. She is my number one priority. Will you help me?"

Vickie was taken aback by the straightforwardness of Agent McGill to the point she was almost speechless.

"What do you want us to do," Bill asked.

Just then, one of the FBI Forensic Team members processing the van called for Agent McGill. They all walked over to it. The back doors to the van were wide open.

"Everything on the outside of the van is clean, including under the hood." the specialist stated "Wiped down just like the manager said he saw the guy doing. Funny thing though, the battery cables and several other wires are unhooked and tied in knots. Why would he do that? I've never seen anything like that. There were no prints found there either."

"That's bloody peculiar. I've never heard of it either."

"The inside is mainly clean too, however, he missed something."

"Did you get a print?" Vickie asked, her eyes wide with anticipation.

The man looked at Agent McGill.

"Go ahead," Tommy said.

"The entire inside was wiped down as well." He turned and with his gloved hands, lifted a box from the back. "It's a first aid kit. It was strapped to the back of the passenger seat. The outside is clean." He turned and put the box down on the floor of the back of the van. He unhooked the clasp and opened the box.

Vickie gasped and put her hand out to Bill's arm.

"Oh, my," Bill exclaimed.

Inside the box were a mostly used roll of white medical tape, several opened and empty packages of large gauze patches, and a pair of blunt-tip scissors. All of which had blood on them. On the inside lid of the box was a very nice set of blood-red fingerprints. Someone forgot to clean the inside of the first aid box after using it to treat a wound.

"Get those processed right away. Check and see if it matches Caution Murphy's blood type. If it's not a match, check it with what was found on her dog. Get a DNA profile and check it on the database."

Agent McGill went over to the restaurant manager again and spoke with him for a few minutes. He came back smiling. "The guy with the van was alone. There were some bandages on his left arm. He was having a lot of problems with it while he was inside and while washing down the van."

"I bet that's where Molly grabbed hold of him, trying to protect Caution," Vickie said. "Good girl, Molly."

"Looks like it. She took a chunk out of him and he used

the first aid kit in the van," Bill said. "But I bet the van's stolen, isn't it Agent McGill?"

"It's not stolen but it is a rental, although the plates have been changed. I have someone getting all the information from the rental company. I have a feeling they used false identification or some unsuspecting person to rent the van. I don't have much hope on the info being good."

"Hopefully, they have video surveillance at the rental," Bill said.

"Something else," Agent McGill continued, "the guy bought three burgers and three sodas. He dropped the bag of sodas trying to get back in the van. That was before he started cleaning it. There's a wet sack on the lot next to the driver's side of the van with three empty cups in it."

"Three burgers and three drinks," Vickie repeated, excitedly. "Caution and the two guys who took her. She's alive! And they're going to keep her alive, otherwise, why feed her?"

"Exactly what we're hoping," McGill said with a smile.

"Did they say if the guy got picked up or was walking?" Bill asked. "Did they give a description?"

"We're getting that information now, we're checking everything," Tommy said.

"I hope so," Vickie said, under her breath.

"What was that, detective?"

"I just hope we are doing everything we can."

"Me too. And in full disclosure, I was hoping you would tell me about what happened at that private investigator's office and what it has to do with this case, "Agent McGill stated.

Bill and Vickie looked at each other.

Over at the far side of the parking lot, Bubba Thompson was sitting on the back end of his flatbed wrecker sipping a very large soda and chewing the last huge bite of a triple-decker burger while he was waiting for instructions. He was afraid Mr. Granger would fire him for sure for not getting the wrecker and the haul back before the next shift.

He looked over and saw the FBI man talking with another man and a woman. Swallowing the oversized bite, he called out. "Hey, I know that guy," he said out loud to no one in particular, pointing at Bill. "He's a detective. I wonder where his short, little partner is?"

Bubba scooted his big butt off the end of the flatbed and landed his big boots with a heavy thump on the pavement of the parking lot. He walked over to the detective and stood there, sucking the end of the soda through the straw, making a very loud and disturbing noise.

Bill couldn't help but notice the big man and turned to him. "May I help you?"

"Hi, detective, remember me? From the police department. I was getting my permit to drive a wrecker. I'm working for Mr. Granger now over at the impound yard."

"Yes," Bill said, not sure of the giant's name. "My grandson, Sam was with me."

"Your grandson? He said he was your partner. I thought he was just a little short, you know, maybe a midget."

Bill shook his head and Vickie quickly put her hand over her mouth to stifle the giggle trying to escape. Agent McGill just turned and walked off to confer with one of his other agents. You could hear him say as he left, "Bloody plonker. The wheels spinning, but the hamster's dead."

"Detective," Bubba said, looking down and shuffling his feet. "I need to ask you for a big favor,"

"Oh? And what can I do for you?" Bill asked.

"Could you call Mr. Granger and tell him why I'm not back yet. It's my first day by myself and I'm not sure he would understand or believe me."

"I think something could be arranged," Bill said.

"And could I bum a couple of dollars, I wanted to get another soda and some fries while I'm waiting."

CHAPTER 18

Five days and almost seventy hard miles later, they were traveling close to the North Platt River, approaching Fort Bernard. This was a small, private, fur trading post on the site of an older fort, abandoned five years earlier just eight miles east of Fort Laramie.

The American Fur Company started by John Joseph Astor owned the trading post which was once to the west of Fort Laramie and relocated in 1846 so they could get the business of the wagon trains before getting to the larger fort. They were also known to under sale Fort Laramie by as much as forty to fifty percent making a big incentive to stop there.

While many of the members of the wagon train were able to stock up on some supplies, some were able to trade in their tired animals for fresh. Usually at around half to three quarters the price of a new one.

One of the traders attempted to acquire Midnight from Patrick, however, Patrick was not about to sell or trade his horse. The trader, armed with several knives and two flintlock pistols stuck in his belt, was trying to intimidate Patrick, offering what he called a more than a fair price, waving a deerskin bag of coins in Patrick's face. He backed down when Big Mike stepped in and made sure he understood the word, 'NO'.

There were no more incidents and the decision was made to stay in the area and to head for Fort Laramie in the morning. Otherwise, they might be getting there in the dark which was never a good idea.

With the wagons in their usual formation, Patrick and Mike fed and watered the animals, greased and tightened the wagon wheels, ate a hearty dinner, and got ready to turn in. Their normal routine didn't vary too often.

The campfire burned itself down to glowing embers and Mike, close to the fire, was dead asleep. Patrick stayed up to write in his journal but finally succumbed to his falling eyelids. He was asleep under the wagon when something brought him fully awake. He didn't move. He heard some rustling but didn't think it would be a wild animal and he didn't think it would be Indians. They were quieter than that. If it were Indians, the only thing that would wake you up is your screaming as they took your scalp.

He saw Midnight's unhobbled legs, but he also saw a pair of human legs next to them. Legs covered by buckskin. Patrick always kept his pistol close to him and this time it was in a pack with some of his other things that he used as a pillow. He kept it loaded while it was secured in the pack but left the chamber under the hammer empty to keep from having accidents. He pulled it out and held it close to him. He rolled quietly out from under the wagon on the opposite side. He stood and slowly went to the far end of the wagon. He took a quick look and saw the trader who wanted to buy Midnight earlier trying to control the horse, but he wasn't being cooperative.

"Do you need some help?" Patrick asked, stepping from around the end of the wagon.

The trader was surprised and turned quickly, reaching for one of his flintlocks. It was the wrong move. Patrick brought up the big pistol just as the trader cleared his belt, but he never got any further. Patrick was well practiced now and without having to think about what to do, he pulled the hammer back with his thumb as he was bringing it up and pushing the heavy pistol far out in front of him, pulling the trigger all in one move.

Mike almost had a heart attack and jumped up at the loud report, looking all around. Shortly, several people came running, some men even brought their shotguns and rifles asking what was happening, if it were Indians or a bear. Mike went to the other side of the wagon and he saw Patrick with his gun in his hand. At the far end of the wagon was a figure on the ground. It wasn't moving. Next to it was a big flintlock pistol.

"I shot him," Patrick said. "He was trying to steal Midnight and he pulled his pistol on me."

Others who arrived to see what the shot was all about came around and saw the body on the ground. Some women covered their mouths and some men just shook their heads. A few were asking what happened and who was on the ground. Some asked if he were dead.

The wagon master and the lieutenants arrived and told everyone to go back to their wagons. They didn't. The captain took Patrick's pistol from his hand and asked, "Are you okay, son."

"Yes, sir," was all Patrick could tell him right then.

"It was self-defense, captain," Mike said.

"Did you see it?" The wagon master asked.

"Well, no. But Patrick told me what happened."

A man came running from the nearby trading post, he stopped and looked down. "That's my partner, Buckskin Bob." He saw the hole in his chest and knelt beside him, turning him over. A larger hole was in the back of the bloody buckskin shirt. There was no sign of life left in the man.

"Who did this?" The man asked, angrily.

"I did," Patrick said, meekly. "He was trying to steal my horse."

The man rose up and began to charge at Patrick, but Big Mike grabbed him. "Settle down, now. I'm sorry about your friend, but it was his own fault.," Mike said.

"The devil can have him," the man said. "He owed me a lot of money and now I'll never see it."

"We'll need to report this to the right people," the captain said. "Tomorrow when we get to Fort Laramie, I'm going to have to turn you over the military; they have the authority here."

"The military?" Mike said. He heard stories about military justice. "They won't care about the truth. He shot a man. They'll hang him for sure."

"Good, he'll get what he deserves." the trading post owner said.

"Maybe they will," the wagon master said, "but we don't have any other choice. We have a dead man here and no witness. The young man even says he shot him. They'll give him a fair trial. They won't have to wait for a judge."

"If they hang him," the trading agent said. "I should get his horse and all his belongings. It's only right to make up for my loss."

"Your loss? Let me ask you something," the wagon master said. "Did you know your partner was a no good, low down, willing to kill, horse stealing, snake?"

"Well, I, uh—no, of course not," he stammered.

"How do we know you're not partners with him in stolen horse-trading?"

"I'm not, I swear," the man pleaded with his eyes staring wide.

"So, with your partner gone, who are you going to split the profits with from all the sales you made today?"

"I don't have to share them," the man just realized.

"So, it looks like your old partner just paid you back."

111

"Do I still get the horse?" he asked, still trying to work an angle.

"But he was stealing Midnight, Patrick's horse," Mike said. "And he was pulling a bloody gun out on him. He would have killed him too."

"That's what the boy says," The wagon master said. "He can tell the military his story. Where's the horse in question?"

"She ran off after the gunshot," Mike stated. "She's out there," Mike said, pointing into the dark.

"I'd go find him before he gets far, and it gets too late."

"Sorry," the wagon master stated to Patrick, he walked over and picked up the dead man's unfired gun, "but I'm going to have to secure you at my wagon until I can turn you over to the military tomorrow. I'll get a couple of the boys to come get the body. He'll have to go too.

"It's okay, Mike," Patrick said. "I'll be fine. Go find Midnight for me. He's a good horse. I don't want to lose him."

"I'll get a couple of men to come help you," the wagon master said. "You shouldn't be out there in the dark by himself."

The trader still trying to get more than he deserved asked if he could get his old partner's pistols and knives but was told they were going to the fort as evidence. He left, headed back to the trading post while figuring in his head how much he was going to make since he didn't have to share anything now.

The wagon master was right about the horse. Mike and a

couple of the riders found Midnight after about fifteen minutes. He wasn't going to run too far in the dark.

Getting back to the wagon, he secured Midnight, stroking his side to calm him down. Now it was Mike's turn to try and calm down. He knew he wasn't getting back to sleep. There were only a few more hours till daylight anyway. He kept seeing in his mind's eye, poor Patrick dangling at the end of a long rope, but he was also telling himself there was no way he was going to allow that to happen.

The wagon master took Patrick back to his wagon. There, the captain went into a box and pulled out a set of hand irons.

"You won't need those," Patrick stated. "I won't go anywhere."

"I don't think you would, son," the man said, "and I hate to do it, but it's something I got to do. It's only going to be until we get to the fort."

"You don't honestly think they'll hang me, do you?"

"I honestly don't know. The military might want to set an example. There's been a lot of incidents; robbing, stealing, fighting, horse thieving, shooting's, and the military wants to stop it. Last trip I saw a man at one military post hung just for shooting a dog. The dog was chasing some cattle alright and granted, it was the post commander's dog, but hanging a man for shooting a dog, that's a bit rough.

"So, it don't look good?" Patrick's shoulders slumped.

"I'm sorry, son. I wish I could tell you different."

The wagon master put the irons on one of Patrick's wrists and the other on the lower part of a wagon spoke, so he could sit on the ground. He locked them with a key he put into his pocket.

"Can I get you anything?" he asked.

"I'm good," Patrick said, giving a forced smile. "Just do me one favor."

"Sure thing," the wagon master stated.

"Just don't lose that bloody key."

"The wagon master couldn't help but give a short chuckle and shook his head as he walked away.

CHAPTER 19

A sketch artist was called to the scene and was getting information from the manager and the employees of the burger joint. The samples of the blood found in the first aid box were sent to the lab, the bloody fingerprints also found in the box were too wet to transfer, so high-resolution photographs were taken, prints classified, and were being run through records.

Video surveillance recordings from as many cameras around the area from the business still open were having their files being checked by dozens of FBI agents. The rest would be checked first thing in the morning when they opened.

It seemed no rock was being left unturned and if they could, they'd check the underbellies of any snails under those rocks too. Tommy McGill knew he was getting close; they just needed a little more time and a bunch more luck.

There were a lot of places the guy could have gone. He could have caught a ride, jumped on a bus, be dozens of miles from there, or he could be just around the corner or up the street. Why was he at *that* fast-food restaurant? And what the blazes happened to the wires in the van, anyway?

The report on the rented van was called in by one of his agents. He made it there just before they closed. It was rented using false documents. A woman picked it up from the lot and used a credit card and driver's license reported stolen after the truck was rented. No one remembered much about her or what she looked like except she wore a big floppy hat and big sunglasses. Her long hair could have been a wig.

Surveillance cameras at the truck rental picked up someone matching the description, but the hat was always blocking any shot of her face. The video was almost worthless.

"She knows there are video cameras there or she has a face like a bloody busted cabbage," Tommy said.

The sketch artist drew a rough sketch all the witnesses agreed was the man who bought the burgers and was wiping down the van. A more detailed one would be distributed later in the day.

"How soon do you think we'll hear about the blood samples and the fingerprints?" Bill asked. He already knew the answer, it was a way for him to try and hurry the process if he could and to make sure they were going to be notified.

"We should get the fingerprint records back within a couple of hours. We'll get the test results on the blood no later than tomorrow. My people are just about done here. I'm having the van towed over to our secure lot by our office at the Richard Russell Building, for now," Agent McGill said. "I'll let you know when the report comes in. Is there anything else you want to share with me?"

"That's it," Vickie said.

"No. We'll call you if we come across anything," Bill added.

Caution was taken almost eight hours ago and Bill and Vickie were exhausted, but they knew they couldn't stop. Not as long as Caution was still out there, scared, alone, and who knows where.

William N. Gilmore

CHAPTER 20

Sheila Murphy was in bed resting. The family doctor made an emergency house call and gave her a mild sedative. She refused at first, not wanting to be sleeping while Caution was not home, but Sean insisted, noting she was beyond distraught. She was worn out and was not doing herself or anyone else any good. It was already getting late. He promised to get her up if there was any word. She might need the rest now if this were to drag out for any length of time. Sheila didn't have the strength to fight his logic.

FBI agents were still in the dining room waiting for either another call from the kidnappers, information from their labs, or reports from the agents on the street. Waiting and not knowing were the worst parts of the job. Several of the veteran agents knew through this. Sometimes, things worked out, and sometimes, they didn't. Sometimes, the bad guys made mistakes leading the agents right to them, and the victim was rescued and sometimes, just to the victim when it turned into a recovery. And then sometimes no matter what you did, neither was found.

One thing you never did was give up hope. You worked every lead, you followed every clue, and played every angle, no matter how ridiculous it might seem. You analyzed every piece of evidence, talked to every possible witness, believed everyone, and trusted no one. If someone told you, they saw a UFO come down and little green men dressed like Elvis came out of it and took the little girl, you better be on the phone to the Pentagon, NASA, SETI, or some other agency handling these types of reports to verify or refute the information. Nothing goes by without checking; nothing.

Sean Murphy already sent John ahead to prepare and secure all the equipment needed for the hunt of the treasure even before the kidnapping. He expected to join him within the next day or two when the kidnapping occurred.

John was not considered a suspect in Caution's kidnapping although he would be questioned later to see if there might be anything or anyone suspicious he could recall, however, he might be instrumental in helping to get her back.

The demands of the kidnappers were very specific; find the treasure. There was no time to waste if Caution was not found immediately. A small window was still available for diving in the North Atlantic and there was no doubt in Sean's mind they would somehow be followed and watched.

There was no guarantee the treasure would be found, and even if it was, could it be recovered within the timeframe the voice demanded or that during the time, Caution's kidnappers would not do something to his precious little girl. They promised to send her back in a box if he didn't find it.

Sean was willing to do anything, give up everything to get Caution back unharmed. He never thought the family secret would resurface through someone else one day and put the lives of his family in jeopardy. It was more of a family curse coming back to haunt them.

Sean wondered. *What would Great-Grand Father Patrick do?*

Special Agent-in-Charge, Tommy McGill arrived back at the Murphy home. The agent stationed at the front drive opened the gate for him and Tommy drove up to the house. He was bringing news.

Everyone was quiet and held their breath when Agent McGill stepped into the dining room. They could tell he was about to make an announcement.

Sean Murphy was standing, holding onto the corner of the table, waiting to hear. Not sure if he really wanted to and glad his wife was upstairs.

"We're one-hundred percent sure she is alive," Tommy said smiling. "We've recovered evidence they are taking care of Caution, feeding her, at least."

Sean's knees almost buckled, glad for the table support.

"We also recovered the van they used," he continued. "We have physical evidence which has been sent to the lab. Bloody evidence, and I do mean *blood evidence.* It appears the suspect Molly got hold of was bleeding profusely from an arm wound. He tried to clean the van, but he forgot to clean bloody fingerprints in a first aid box in the van."

"How do you know it's not Caution's blood," Sean asked, a little precariously.

"There is no evidence Caution was bleeding at any time. We'll get it checked to be sure, but I am confident it is not hers. In addition, we have witnesses who saw the man. There were bloody bandages on his left arm. We'll have a sketch soon and hopefully an ID."

"Where is he now?" Sean asked. "Was Caution with him?"

"We don't think she was there. No one saw her. As to where the man is now, we don't know. He may have just simply walked away and we're checking the area, but he may have been picked up."

"Why aren't we out there now? Checking every building, every car?" Sean Murphy questioned.

Most places are closed," Tommy said. "We won't have access to a lot of the area and there is a bloody lot of area to cover, even if she is nearby. If we try to saturate the area in the dark, without the right recourses, we could spook them, allow them to get away, or worse, put them in a position where they would harm Caution. We have to do this when it is most beneficial to us. We will know a lot more in the morning as well. Hopefully, their names, which will go a long way in maybe telling us about them and where they are."

Sean nodded. He understood. He didn't want to do anything that might put Caution in any more danger. He just wanted to do something. He wanted to go and bring his little girl safely home.

One of the other FBI agents spoke up. "Sir. The van was rented by a white female, identity unknown, using a stolen credit card and a Georgia driver's license belonging to the credit card holder. Her purse was stolen. I have a theory that the owner of those cards may look like our suspect, so she could get away with it easier. She may have targeted the victim to steal her identity."

"You may have a good point there, Agent Oaks. Work on that angle. What about the stolen plate on the van?"

"It was taken off a similar vehicle parked at Hartsfield-Jackson International Airport and not noticed until the owner returned from Michigan. There was a window of about a week for when the theft occurred. There were no working surveillance cameras in the area, but I'm checking more into why."

"So, all the information we have right now shows this was planned for a good week or more in advance. Which means they will have a place set up for stashing of the van, Caution, and themselves for a while. But something went wrong with the van and it was left at the hamburger place. If our suspect walked, how far would he have walked?"

Agent Oaks unfolded a large paper map of the Atlanta area and spread it out on the table. She grabbed a red pen. She circled Jim's, the van rental location, and the airport.

Lifting the map and searching under it for a few seconds, she located the paper she was looking for. Checking the police report on the stolen credit card and license, she circled the theft location on the map. She then connected all the small circles with one big one. She looked up at Agent McGill smiling. "Sir, I believe they are still somewhere in this area," she said, handing him the map.

"I want surveillance teams out in this area ten bloody minutes ago," Agent McGill boomed out. "We don't have much to go on, I know. As soon as we get a sketch, a photo, an ID, or anything tangible, we'll get it out to you. I want agents in place watching, looking, and scrutinizing anything that looks suspicious. Unless you see Caution and she is in imminent danger, do not confront or approach any suspect. We know there are at least two and we want to get them both at one time, alive if possible, and without putting Caution in any jeopardy. That being said, our number one priority is to get Caution back, quickly and safely, and without anyone getting hurt."

Several of the agents quickly got on their phones calling surrounding police jurisdictions which may be in the area where Caution could be. Also, a request was made for extra manpower for all the eyes they would need.

"Agent Oaks," Tommy called her out, "how would you like to lead the surveillance detail?"

"Yes, sir. I'd like that very much, sir."

"Bring me back some good intelligence and help me find that little girl." Agent McGill told her.

"Yes, sir."

Tommy was almost afraid she was about to salute him. The former Marine, a combat intelligence officer, was only out of the academy for about a year, but she was good, very good. It was time to let her loose in the field. "Just get me someone here who can run all this equipment and the computer work we need. And stop calling me sir."

"Yes, sir, I mean no, sir. I—I have just the person in mind. I'll have him here in thirty minutes, Si..." she stopped before she started to say it again. Red-faced, she turned and jumped on her phone.

In twenty-five minutes, a young man carrying a large briefcase came into the Murphy house and after being stopped and showing his FBI credentials for the third time, he was directed to the dining room.

Tommy was talking with another agent when the young man walked up to them. Tommy looked at the kid. "May I help you, lad?"

"I'm Azira Hazar," he said. "I'm here to help with the tech and any computer work you have."

"I'm sorry, are you even out of high school yet?" Tommy quipped, surprised at the youthfulness of the lad. The other agent just smiled.

"I've graduated college," he stated. "I started MIT while I was still fourteen."

Agent Oaks came up to them. "I see you've met my friend Azira," she said, putting her arm around him. "Don't let his young age fool you. He's the best there is when it comes to computers. Did he tell you he just graduated from MIT? He's so good, he's known as the Magician."

"Is he now, we were just talking about it before he said he needed to get to bloody work. I can see he's going to be quite the asset."

CHAPTER 21

The wagon master fixed Patrick a biscuit with a big slab of bacon for a quick breakfast. Patrick didn't get much sleep. Not so much worry as it was being shackled to the wagon wheel all night. There was no way to get comfortable and every move made too much noise.

Mike didn't get a bit of sleep. He took care of all the early morning chores himself without fixing any breakfast, He wasn't hungry. Which in itself was testimony as to how he was feeling.

It would take a long three or four hours to get to Fort Laramie. Every foot would have Mike thinking about Patrick's fate at the hands of the hangman. He didn't know how to help his friend. He could lie to the judge and say he saw the trapper pull his gun first, but he already told the wagon master he didn't see what happened.

He could go bust Patrick out of the shackles and they could make a run for it on Midnight, but that would make Patrick look guilty for sure. They would both be wanted then and if caught they both might hang. That would be the end of their gold quest. No castle by the ocean. No future of any kind.

Mike needed to wait and let him take his chances with the

court. He must show somehow it was self-defense and hope they believed him. There was the chance the court didn't care. Hangings were the ultimate entertainment. It was a public gathering, a picnic, and a build-up to an exciting, yet gruesome finish, where there was little else to break the day to day routine and boredom. The military courts didn't want to disappoint, and they usually didn't.

Justice was also dispatched quickly. With the military having jurisdiction, the commanding officer or his designee was the judge, an officer was the lawyer for the accused while another was the prosecutor. Troopers were chosen as the jury and one as the executioner. They didn't have to wait for a territorial judge, and everything usually took less than a day or two from the start of the trial to hanging.

The owner of the trading post also went along to make sure Patrick would meet his fate at the end of a rope and to try and get the judge to award him Midnight and Patrick's other belongings as compensation. He didn't make too many friends along the way and stayed to himself. He especially kept clear of Mike.

Patrick remained shackled and in the back of the wagon on the trip to Fort Laramie. He did not have a comfortable ride.

There were several shouts when the fort came into view. The fort itself was nothing more than a few buildings close to each other. Soldiers were milling about, some appeared to be on guard duty. Around the fort were teepees, lean-tos, and rough shacks. There were quite a few Indians camped around the fort as well as several wagons and corrals for different animals such as horses, oxen, mules, and livestock.

Fort Laramie replaced an older establishment at the same location known as Fort John. Not a real fort, it served as a place migrant travelers could stop and rest. In 1849, old Fort John was purchased by the U. S. Army and commissioned a military fort. The garrison consisted of several cavalry companies and Company G, 6th US Infantry.

Upon arrival, the wagon master asked to see the commanding officer. He was directed to his office with the trader insisting on going as well.

"I have a prisoner who shot and killed a man," the wagon master stated to the officer. "He says it was in self-defense when the man trying to steal his horse pulled a gun on him the other night."

"He murdered him, major" the trader stated flatly. "It was Buckskin Bob," he said, aware the major knew him.

"So, Bob's been shot dead. No big loss. Do you have anyone who saw this?" The officer asked.

"No," the wagon master declared.

"See," the trader said. "He shot Bob in cold blood."

"Why would he do that? The major asked.

"I don't know," the trader said. "Maybe he was drunk,

or they mixed words. Maybe it was a bad trade. What difference does it make? He killed Bob. He needs to hang."

"You have authority over this, major," the wagon master said. "I can't keep my wagons here while you hold a trial. I have to get them over the mountains before the snows."

"Where's the prisoner now? The commanding officer asked.

"He's in my wagon."

"Lieutenant Harris," the major yelled out.

A young man in uniform opened the door and marched to the major's desk, stopped, and saluted. "Sir?"

"Take charge of the wagon master's prisoner and put him in the stockade. Looks like we're going to have us a trial and a hanging."

"Yes sir," the young man said with a big smile.

"And get statements from anyone who knows anything and who can write or get it written up for them and have them put their mark on it. The wagons have to leave soon."

"Yes, Sir," the young man saluted again. He did a sharp about-face and followed the wagon master and the trader out of the major's office. The trader wore a smile on his face as well while the wagon master wondered if he made a mistake bringing Patrick to the fort.

CHAPTER 22

Caution was sitting in the box asleep. The top was closed. As bad as she wanted to stay awake, she couldn't keep her eyes open any longer. Even with the tape around her ankles and her hands, and with her knees pulled up to her chin, she found a position where things didn't hurt as much.

Roger was keeping watch while Quin was trying to fit his body on a worn-out mattress on a short, metal bed frame not too far away. Even with his arm aching, he slept like a log and was snoring loudly. Two more hours of this and Roger would wake him for his turn at the watch. Two more hours of snoring and farting. Quin was a piece of work. The girl was fast asleep as well. Thank goodness she didn't snore.

Roger needed to go pee. He didn't want to wake up Quin just for that. The girl was asleep, and she was taped up. The top of the box was closed. Quin would never know. He headed for the bathroom.

"Caution. Caution, wake up, sweetheart."

Caution opened her eyes even though she couldn't see through the hood or out of the box. It was dark. Someone was calling to her. It wasn't either of the two men. It was a voice she knew.

"Grandpa?" She said softly. "Grandpa, I'm here."

"Yes, my little darling. So am I."

"These men took me from home. They hurt Molly. Are Mom and Dad alright?"

"Yes, they love and miss you. They have everyone looking for you, including your police friend Vickie."

"Grandpa, I want to go home."

"And you will, very soon, my dear. I have some things I have to do to help them find you."

"How did you find me, Grandpa?"

"I always know where you are, my dear. Our special bond is strong, stronger than I've experienced with anyone else. There are a few, for some reason I can't explain, who I can interact with, but they can't see or hear me as you do."

"You're not going to leave me, are you?" A little whimper escaped her lips.

"I hate to do it, but I have to somehow show them the way. I can't just tell them or write them a note on a piece of paper. It's not like that. There appear to be limits as to what I can do. I hope it won't be long. I know you're not comfortable in that box. I know how you feel. I was a prisoner once myself and it's not fun. I know it's scary and hard to deal with, but believe me, I'm going to do everything I can to help get your friends to find you as soon as possible."

"Okay Grandpa, I believe you. Is Molly okay? Did she

get hurt bad?"

"She's going to be fine. She's a tough dog and she also loves and misses you. That gives me an idea. I think I may know a way for them to find you. We're going to need some special help though."

"I love you, Grandpa. I don't want you to leave."

"I love you too, my treasure. I don't want to leave you here all alone with these men. But I must go so I can bring you help. I want you to be strong like I know you can be."

"I understand, Grandpa. I'll be strong. I'm trying to think what you and Vickie would do if you were here. I'm listening and learning and now I have a lot of information for Vickie about them. I'm trying to be a good detective just like both of you."

"I'm so proud of you, Caution. Everything is going to be fine and you'll be home soon with your Mom and Dad, and Molly too. I promise."

"And with you."

"Yes, with me too," he said, his ghostly voice cracking a bit.

"Hey, little girl, are you talking in your sleep?" Roger called out. "Do I need to put tape over your mouth too?"

Caution didn't say anything further. She could feel Grandpa Patrick was no longer present. A tear slowly fell down her cheek.

CHAPTER 23

Patrick was put into the fort's stockade. It was more of a room with a locked door and a guard. At least the shackles came off. Patrick was told the commanding officer would meet with him shortly, tell him what was going to happen and when.

Mike went to the fort and asked if he could see Patrick. The guard stated it would be up to the major and to come back later. Mike knew the wagon train would continue in a day or so and time was not on their side. If Patrick was found guilty, he'd never leave Fort Laramie. He'd be hung and buried in their cemetery. A marker might stay up for a year or two, but at some point, no one would know who was buried there and Patrick's little place on the prairie would be forgotten. Maybe not by Mike, but Mike wasn't going to stay there forever, and it was a good bet he wouldn't be returning to the area.

Mike went and checked with the wagon master and after some long deliberations, he agreed to wait two days before leaving. Giving the animals a rest and allowing others to get the supplies they needed for the next push was as good an excuse as any. They did not want to blame the delay on one person.

After several hours, the commanding officer finally went to meet with Patrick. He was now a distraction more than a priority.

At the stockade, the officer went in to talk with Patrick, unarmed, of course, and with little hope of a good outcome for the young man.

"So, you're the one who shot Buckskin Bob. Not much to look at, are you?"

"Yes, I shot him," Patrick admitted. "He was trying to steal my horse and I surprised him. He drew his gun on me. What choice did I have? Let him shoot me?"

"And you have how many people who saw this who are willing to tell that story?"

"It was just me and him," Patrick stated. "It was late at night or early morning. Everyone was asleep. There was a noise that woke me up and I saw someone trying to take my horse. He unhobbled Midnight and put a bridle on him. I snuck around the wagon and confronted him while he was trying to take my horse. He drew one of his pistols from his belt and I was carrying my gun in my hand. I shot him before he could shoot me."

"But that's what you say. Bob can't tell me his story. No one can tell me if that's what happened or not."

"I'm telling you. That's what happened. I swear."

"Tomorrow, I'll have one of my officers come and talk with you. We'll get this trial started while we have some free time. The wagon train will need to head out in a day or two. I don't think you're going to be going with them. It's not looking too good for you, son. I'd start saying some prayers and getting things together in your mind and with your soul if you need to. Do you have any family with you?"

"My mind is straight, and my soul is right," Patrick stated. "I don't have any family here. I'd like to see my partner, Mike, if you don't mind."

"We'll arrange it. There's not going to be any problem with you, is there?"

"No, sir. I just want to tell my story. My true story" Patrick said.

The major went back to his office where Buckskin Bob's partner was waiting for him.

"Buckskin Bob was my friend for a long time. That boy shot him and took him away from me. Bob did all my supply runs for me. Now I'm out a partner, time, and money. I think it would be only right if I were to take the boy's horse and property to cover my losses."

"Bob was an ass and he stole from you. You know it, I know it, almost everybody knows it. The boy did you a favor."

"Be that as it may, I'm still owed compensation. I'm losing money right now just being here."

"Go back to the trading post then. We don't need you here."

"I came to get what I'm owed. It's only fair."

"Why don't you wait until the trial's over? He may not be

found guilty."

"That's funny. When was anyone not found guilty of murder when they shot someone in cold blood?"

"It will look better if you wait. I'll rule on it just as soon as he's found guilty. We're starting the trial tomorrow."

"Well, okay then, tomorrow it is. I want to get back to the trading post with the horse while the boy's still kicking at the end of the rope."

"Get out of my office," the major said, pointing to the door. "You disgust me."

Mike went again to see if he could get to visit with Patrick. This time, he was allowed in the shack with him.

"Keep your head up, Patrick," Mike said, trying to do the same. You'll come out of this like—"

"No. Not this time." Patrick cut him off. "It's not going to be okay. I want you to go with the wagon train to California. I want you to find all the gold and build that castle."

"I'm not leaving you," Mike said, shocked that Patrick would even think of that "We're in this together. We're partners."

"Till death do us part," Patrick added.

"Longer," Mike said, a tear growing in his eye. "I'll think of something. I'll get you out of here."

"Mike," Patrick said softly, looking the big man in the eyes. "Thank you for bringing me on this journey, but I think this is as far as I'm supposed to go. I don't want you doing nothing stupid. I'll face the jury. What happens, happens. The only thing I ask is I don't want that man getting Midnight. Set her free if you must. It's not right."

"He'll never lay a bloody hand on her, I promise," Mike said.

"Thank you. You're a good partner and a better friend," Patrick said.

Neither of them could stop the tears.

CHAPTER 24

Special Agent Tommy McGill was trying to make sense of everything going on with Gerald Olson; Tanner, his dead investigator; the girl, most likely his killer, found in their offices; Dearing; millions in sunken gold treasure; and the kidnapping of the little Murphy girl.

And although the murder suspect who called herself Teri Mason and was later identified as Terry Kline, denied any knowledge about the kidnapping, he wanted to find out himself. He didn't believe in coincidences. He wanted her in his interrogation room within the hour.

He got one of his agents to secure a court order to have her transferred to the FBI Field Office in Atlanta for further questioning. Lieutenant Cummings was not happy when he received the call to get her ready to turn over. She was in his custody for murder. She was their suspect. And although she lawyered up, he was sure after a few hours in the room with no rest, or food, she might change her mind and decide she wanted to talk after all; to him. But there was a court order he could not refuse. However, there were a few things he could do. He let the FBI know they needed to come get her. He wasn't going to tie up his people to transport her. They got the court order; they could come get her.

Two FBI agents arrived within a half-hour and produced a copy of the court order. They took Kline into their custody, handcuffing her, and taking her to the secured parking lot where she was placed in the back-right passenger seat of a big, black SUV. One agent, a female, sat in the back with her while the other drove them to the FBI office.

It was only a couple of miles and there was barely any traffic being so late. They made a stop at a red light on Spring Street and just as the light turned green and they started across the intersection, a big truck slammed into the front driver's side of the SUV.

The agent driving was knocked unconscious, the airbags were deployed but the sheer force of the impact took its toll. The agent in back, although badly shaken and slow to respond, released her seatbelt and tried to open the back door. It was jammed and would not open for her. She then began to check on the prisoner as she crawled over her to the other side to the passenger side door.

Just as she reached for it, it opened wide. The agent looked up only to see something blurry coming at her before she felt the blow to her forehead. She dropped unconscious onto the lap of Kline.

A man with gloved hands reached in and lifted the agent off her, shoving her limp body back over to the other side of the vehicle, he then flipped open a knife and cut the seatbelt holding Kline in and helped get her out of the SUV and onto her feet in the roadway. "Are you alright?" He asked, holding onto her, making sure she was steady enough to stand on her own.

"I am now."

He took a small, silver-colored key and unlocked the handcuffs, removing them from her wrists, tossing them back into the FBI's mangled car.

With her arms now free, she stood on her tiptoes and wrapped them around the neck of the man. "Thanks, uncle.

The man looked around to see if there were any witnesses needing to be dealt with. "It's clear. Let's get out of here," he said with a smile.

Another car with a driver was waiting for them and once they were in the back, it sped away into the night.

CHAPTER 25

The morning sun was just peeking over the horizon as Patrick sat in the corner of the small room when the door opened. A young man in a clean, dark-blue uniform came in.

"I'm Lieutenant Harris. I'll be your legal counsel for the trial in a couple of hours," he stated, handing Patrick a bowl of soup with bits of meat and a piece of bread.

"Thank you," Patrick said. "No spoon?"

The lieutenant looked at him and smiled. "Sorry, not allowed."

"You're not much older than I am; have you done this before?"

"No. This is the first time, but my father was a judge. I've only been assigned here for about a month. I was at Fort Bridger, but they needed a replacement. I understand you shot someone, killed them, but you don't have any witnesses."

"He was stealing my horse late at night and he pulled a gun on me. Everyone else was asleep. Should I have let him shoot me?"

"It might have been easier to show he pulled a gun on you."

"His gun was on the ground next to him. When I shot the

trader, my horse ran off, everyone showed up after," Patrick explained.

"I'll have a couple of troopers come to get you when it's time. Is there anything you want in the meantime?"

Patrick handed the lieutenant the empty bowl. "Would it be okay if my partner brought my journal and a pencil?"

"I'll have it taken care of," the young man stated in a solemn voice as he left, knowing there was little he was going to be able to do to keep the rope off the youth's neck.

About an hour later, Mike showed up with the journal as requested. He was allowed to stay with Patrick while waiting for the trail to begin. Not much was said between them as Patrick wrote for a while, looked up, smiled, and wrote some more. This went on for another hour or so when two of the garrison troopers arrived.

They put hand irons and leg chains on Patrick and escorted him out of the stockade. As they walked him towards one of the main buildings, they passed a crudely built gallows. An old, weathered rope with a noose tied into it was swinging in the wind.

"Don't worry," one of the guards stated, "we'll put a new rope up to hang you with."

"We wouldn't want it to break and have you fall to your death," the other laughed.

A group of people; Indians, travelers, and a few soldiers

started to gather and sit around the old gallows in anticipation of the show which was sure to come very shortly. They wanted to get the best view. The trials usually didn't take too long and the hangings were carried out before the sun began its burning march across the sky.

When they got to the main building, they passed two troopers guarding the entrance. Inside, Patrick saw tables and chairs set up facing a desk. Lieutenant Harris was sitting at one of the tables with an empty chair next to him and there was another military officer Patrick did not recognize sitting at the other table.

Patrick was taken to the table with Lieutenant Harris and was helped to sit down in the chair beside him.

"I'll do my best," the lieutenant said, not looking Patrick in the eyes, "but I can't promise anything. Just tell the truth."

"I always have," Patrick returned.

To the right of Patrick's table were twelve chairs; six in front and six in back. There were chairs to the left of the other table as well. In one of those chairs was the man from the trading post.

Mike was directed to one of the chairs, but he didn't take the one next to the trader. As he passed him, he gave him a look of contempt. If he could have gotten away with it, he might have grabbed him by the throat.

An Orderly Sergeant sitting at a table next to the desk

was writing something down. When he finished, he stood and ordered everyone to rise.

The commanding officer of the fort walked into the room from an adjacent one and went to the desk and sat down.

"Orderly Sergeant, have you made a jury selection?"

"That I have, sir, twelve good, bright lads," he said in a strong Irish brogue.

Patrick couldn't help but smile at his countryman.

"Bring in the jury," the major said.

Twelve of the garrison troopers, one a sergeant, came in from the door behind him. He couldn't turn very well, but they marched past him and they all stood by the empty chairs. The sergeant was at the one closest to the commanding officer.

Take your seats," the major said. In unison, they all sat.

"Today we hold trial for the death of," he turned to the trader. "Do you know his real name?"

The trader shook his head. "That's all I've ever known him by."

"The death of Buckskin Bob," the major continued. "Have the defendant rise and state his name and how he pleads."

Lieutenant Harris told Patrick to stand and tell his name and to say he's not guilty.

"My name is Patrick Murphy. I'm not guilty." He sat back down.

"Buffalo crap!" The trader called out. There were a few

chuckles.

Mike glared at the trader and started to rise from his seat.

"Order!" The major boomed out. "There will be no other outbursts in this proceeding unless you want to spend a couple of nights in the stockade. That goes for anyone," he said, looking at Mike.

The orderly sergeant was writing like crazy trying to keep up with everything being said while trying not to laugh himself.

"Lieutenant Anderson, are you ready to present your opening remarks against the defendant?"

"I am, sir," Lieutenant Anderson said.

"Lieutenant Harris, are you ready with your defense?

"I am, sir."

"Lieutenant Anderson, begin," the major said, sitting back in his chair.

Standing and approaching the jury, Lieutenant Anderson began. "Major, members of the jury, and to the court, the defendant, Patrick Murphy, two nights ago, shot and killed Buckskin Bob without provocation. He shot him once in the chest from just a few feet away, killing him instantly. There were no witnesses to the shooting, however, when others arrived, he still held his killing gun in his hand. I have the wagon master of his group to testify to this. He's the one who took the gun away from the cold-blooded killer. I also have his grieving partner, Mr. Isiah Carpenter, here to tell you about his heartfelt personal loss, the costly loss to his business, and the kind and gentle nature of Bob. Don't let the youthful look of this lad fool you. He's a killer. Thank you."

"Thank you, Lieutenant Anderson. Lieutenant Harris, we're ready to hear what you have to say."

"I'm going to waive my opening, at this time your honor."

Lieutenant Anderson smiled, but not as big as the trapper, Isiah Carpenter.

CHAPTER 26

Bill and Vickie wanted to keep looking, but they didn't know where to look or exactly what clues they were looking for in the middle of the night. They finally agreed they needed to get some rest and start again fresh in the morning. Or at least as fresh as possible. They headed back to Bill's house.

Vickie called Special Agent McGee and told him they hit a brick wall, both in ideas and in stamina. He didn't tell them the news about narrowing down the search or the escape of Terry Kline. He was afraid they would keep going and that might be more dangerous than anything. Tired and sleepy agents made mistakes or failed to see things they should. He'd tell them in the morning.

When Bill and Vickie arrived at the house, it was already going on three o'clock. Four or five hours of sleep, a hot shower, and some food would be what they needed to tackle the next round of searches. Hopefully, when they got back to the Murphy's, if Caution hadn't been found yet, there would be some photos and info on the kidnappers.

Bill was fresh out of the shower. He needed that before climbing into bed. He let Vickie go first so as not to use up all the hot water.

Bill was having problems falling asleep. It was difficult knowing there was a little girl out there somewhere in the hands of men who could be so cold as to cause her harm. He wondered if Vickie was getting any sleep herself.

Bill somehow found the allusive niche where he was able to fall into a troubled sleep. His brain finally succumbing to the need to rejuvenate itself from all the day's emotions, activities, and information overload.

He was in a dream state where he was frantically looking for something, something very close, but it continued to elude him, just out of his reach. His hand was reaching into a fog and he knew he was just inches from grabbing the fleeting thing, the thing he so desperately needed.

The fog slowly cleared, and he saw the little Murphy girl so close and he was telling her to reach out, to take his hand, and he stretched, trying to touch her. But the little girl pulled her hand back. "It's not me you want right now," she said, and the image changed.

The little girl was replaced with the image of his wife. Bill wanted to grab her so bad and she started to hold her hand up but pulled it back and told him with a loving smile, "It's not me you need anymore."

He made a great effort to grab the hand and finally, he got a firm hold on the hand reaching out to him. The image changed once again. This time he saw Vickie. It was Vickie he was able to grab and was pulling to him.

"It's me, Bill," she said. "It's been me for a long time."

Bill's phone was ringing. It brought him back to reality quickly and the dream was gone like flash paper in the hands of a magician.

He checked to see who the caller was and was surprised to see it was his daughter, Jenny.

"Hey, what's up, kiddo?"

"Is Sam at your house? Is he with you?" She asked desperately.

"Here? No. Why? What's going on?"

"Dad, he's missing. He's not in his room. He's not in the yard or anywhere around. I called for him and checked the area. He's not supposed to be out of the house without telling me."

"Did something happen. Did you have an argument? Did he run away?"

"No. He's just gone."

"Does it look like any force was used on any of the doors?"

"No. and nothings missing. Nothing's been disturbed."

"Call 9-1-1. I'm on the way."

Bill went to Vickie's room and knocked on the door. She opened it wearing a short robe and a questioning look. When she saw Bill's face, she got a bad feeling deep inside.

"Is there news?" she asked with dread.

153

"My daughter just called. Sam's missing."

"Oh, my God." She was scared to ask the question burning suddenly in her brain.

"It might be them," Bill said, completing the terrible thought. "I need to get to my daughter's house."

"Give me just two minutes to get dressed. I'm coming too." She closed the door part way, not worrying about modesty, as she got dressed.

Bill turned his back to the door. "Thanks. I could use your help if you're up to it."

After just a minute, she came out of the room. "I'll call McGill while you drive us to your daughter's," she said while buttoning up her blouse "We'll find him, we'll find them both."

*

Sam was already in bed when something interrupted his sleep. Something not quite a dream, yet something seemingly real and right there in the room with him. Like when his mother is trying to get him up when he oversleeps for school.

It was a voice. A man's voice. And it was telling him Caution was in trouble and needed him. It told Sam to wake up and to go find Caution.

Sam woke up. He dreamed some strange things in the past; monsters, aliens, superheroes, and the like, but this one stayed with him after he woke while others seemed to fade right away.

It was still early, the sun just having come up and although he didn't have school, he decided to get up now anyway. He rubbed his eyes and needed to go to the bathroom. He was still in his pajamas and while heading down the hallway, he thought twice about going back to bed.

He went into the bathroom and finished, not flushing yet, so he would not make too much noise. He washed his hands and turned to wipe them on a towel when the toilet flushed on its own. He turned and looked at it, thinking maybe he was sleepier than he thought and pushed the handle as a force of habit.

Suddenly, the bathroom became extremely cold and the large mirror over the sink seemed to frost over. Sam stood there looking and started to shiver, icy vapor came out with each breath. He tried to reach for the far away doorknob when he heard screeching at the mirror and slowly turned, barely looking out the corners of his eyes, not certain he wanted to see what was making the fearsome noise. As he watched in horror, letters appeared on the mirror.

Wide-eyed and frozen in fear, he saw letter after letter appear with the sound of the screeching as when you are rubbing wet glass with your bare hand. The letters formed words and Sam held his breath as the words struck home.

It was the same as he heard from the voice during the dream in his nice, warm bed; *"Caution needs you. Find her"*.

Sam was able to get to the door and flew out without

even closing the door. He went straight to his room and jumped under his covers. He thought about running to his mother, but he was afraid she wouldn't believe him. He didn't want to look like a baby, and he didn't want to look like he was crazy either.

Caution was his friend. The man said she needed help. He didn't know why or where. He finally got the courage to get up and head back to the bathroom. The door was still open, and he slowly walked along the wall of the hallway towards the room. He didn't see anyone, and it was no longer freezing.

He got to the door and slowly poked his head in. Nothing. No one was in the bathroom and it was just the way it always looked. He even checked behind the door and then behind the shower curtain. No one was there.

Now, he wondered if he may have dreamed the whole thing. If he was asleep when he thought he got up. He recalled having some pretty realistic dreams before. Some would even cause him to run get in bed with his mom. But that was when he was much younger.

Sam wasn't going to go back to bed, and he wasn't going to wake his mom. He started the shower and went back to his room to get a change of clothes. He even tried laughing at himself. He was up for the day.

The shower was hot and steamy, just the way he liked it. It was refreshing, especially after having the chilling experience.

After cleaning himself, he turned off the water and

reached out and grabbed a towel. He dried his hair, head, and shoulders well and stepped out onto the bathmat. The room was still steam filled. He dried the rest of himself and put on his underwear.

He moved to the mirror ready to wipe it clean, so he could brush his hair. Sam stared in disbelief at the mirror not believing what he was seeing. On the mirror, the steam created a wet, foggy film except where some of the words appeared before. Once more, a message was staring back at him. *"Find her."*

CHAPTER 27

"If that is how you want to proceed, lieutenant," the major said, surprised. "I can't tell you how to defend your client, but I would think you would use every minute, every way possible to try and save him from hanging."

"That is my determination, your honor," the young officer said.

"Lieutenant Anderson, call your first witness."

"Thank you, your honor. I call Brice Newman, wagon master of the defendants traveling group."

Brice Newman took a seat in a chair to the jury's side of the major's desk. He put his hand on a bible and swore to tell the truth.

"Did you see the defendant shoot Buckskin Bob?"

"No. I told you I didn't."

"Yes, I know," Lieutenant Anderson stated. We just have to tell the jury. Do you know anyone who did?"

"No."

"Did you see the defendant with a gun in his hand after you heard the shot?"

"Yes. The lad said he shot him. He was tryin—"

"We'll get to that," Lieutenant Anderson interrupted.

"How many shots did you hear?"

"Just one."

"How many holes were in Bob?"

"Just one. One big one."

"Where was he shot?"

"Next to the wagon."

"No. I mean what part of his body."

"In the chest. I think the heart."

"Was Buckskin Bob dead?"

"Yep. Deader than a rock."

"Did you take a gun from the defendant's hand?"

"Yes."

"Had a shot been fired from that gun?"

"Yes."

"Was a horse there when you got there?"

"No. I was told—"

"Did Buckskin Bob have a gun or a knife in his hand?"

"When?"

"When you found him dead."

"There was—"

"Just yes or no," the lieutenant interrupted once again.

"No."

"That's all I have of this witness, your honor."

"Thank you, Lieutenant Anderson," the major said.

"Lieutenant Harris, your witness."

"Thank you. Mr. Newman, was another gun found?"

"Yes."

"Where was the other gun found?"

"It was on the ground next to Bob's body."

"Did you recover the gun?"

"Yes."

"Had it been fired?"

"No."

"Have you ever seen the gun you recovered before then?"

"Yes."

"It's okay, Mr. Newman, you can elaborate. You don't have to just say yes or no to me."

"Okay. What does elab…what's that mean?" he asked, confused.

"It means you can tell me your whole story without just having to say just yes or no."

"Good. The boy shot Bob because he was stealing his horse and the kid outdrew him."

"Objection, your honor. Facts not in evidence."

"Those are the facts," Newman said.

"He's saying no one saw it happen," the major said. "You can't tell what you believe happened if you didn't see what happened."

"Everyone knows it, even the horse. He was there when it happened."

There were some quiet laughs.

"That's called hearsay," the major told him. "You can't tell us what others have said to you unless they are here in court."

"Even the horse?"

Again, there was laughter.

"Settle down," the major warned. "Enough about the horse. Objection sustained."

"Tell us, Mr. Newman, before you recovered the gun next to Buckskin Bob's body, where was it you saw it before?"

"In Buckskin Bob's belt. He didn't go anywhere without his knives and guns. The guns were a matched set of walnut-stocked flintlocks Bob wanted made just for him."

"How long have you known Buckskin Bob?"

"The three or four trips I've made on this trail. I only saw him at and around the trading post. It was hard to strike a fair deal with him. He always wanted more. The animals he sold were still on the mend, not having enough time to recoup their full strength before he turned them around for sale. They might have been better than what the party brought in, but not by much. He was a hard drinker too."

"Objection," Lieutenant Anderson stated. "He only saw him several times during those three or four trips. He can't say he was always a hard drinker or he carried guns everywhere he went."

"Sustained," the major advised. "Continue."

"Have you experienced any problems out of Patrick Murphy on the trail?"

"Not one. He has been very helpful. He and his partner both," he said, looking first at Patrick then over at Mike.

"Do you think Patrick Murphy should hang for shooting Buckskin Bob?"

"No. Absolutely not. He was in his rights."

"Thank you. I'm done with this witness, your honor," Lieutenant Harris stated.

"You may step down," the major stated.

The wagon master stood and looked down. "That's funny, step down when there ain't no steps," he said as he walked back over to a chair.

"Your honor, I call Isiah Carpenter to the stand." Lieutenant Anderson said.

"The trader stood and walked to the chair. He was stopped by a trooper who held out a Bible for him to put his hand on and swear.

"I don't like to swear," the man said.

"You ain't swearing like cussing," the trooper said, "you're swearing like a promise to tell the truth."

"Well, okay then," he said a little unsteadily as he put his shaking hand on the Bible, "I promise to tell the truth."

"Good enough. Go ahead Lieutenant Anderson," the

major stated.

"How long was Bob your partner?"

"Going on near five years now."

"What all did he do for you?"

"He was my supply train. He brought in everything we sold."

"What do you sell at the trading post?"

"We have a little of everything. Guns, ammo, knives, blankets, horse tack, wagon parts, clothes, food, gold pans, picks, axes, flour, salt, bacon. We have whatever you need and want. And we're cheaper than Fort Laramie."

"With Bob gone, how are you going to get your supplies?"

"I don't know. Bob knew what supplies were on hand and what we needed. He was the only one I knew who would make those trips without it costing me an arm and a leg. He could talk with the Indians too."

"Is this going to hurt your business?"

"Of course."

"Are you going to lose money?"

"A lot of it. I think I should get compensated for my loss. I think I should get the horse, saddle, bridle, and any equipment owned by this cold-blooded killer of my poor partner."

Mike was only half-listening when the trader started, but something caught his ear. He thought for a bit and his eyes went wide. He shot up out of the chair and ran to the doors. Everyone looked at him as he left the building.

Patrick was afraid Mike may have gotten his fill of this proceeding and couldn't stand it anymore. He didn't blame him. He wished he could run out too. He wondered if he would see him again before he got hung.

CHAPTER 28

Molly was examined by the veterinarian and found not to have a concussion or any other major injuries but was kept overnight just to make sure. Early the next morning she was cleared to go home.

The officer who transported her to the vet the day before took pictures of her with the blood in her coat. It was quickly determined to have most likely come from one of the suspects when it was typed as human blood and failed to match Caution's blood type. Samples of the blood was collected and were turned over to the FBI to see if there was any matching identification in the database.

The officer arrived early and was standing at the receptionist desk when the vet brought Molly out to the waiting room. She sat at the officer's feet waiting while the officer and the vet spoke. The officer was about to put a leash on her to take her out to his patrol car when a lady carrying a sickly and sad looking English Bulldog opened the front door. As soon as she did, Molly took off running between her legs almost knocking her down.

The officer tried running after her but couldn't keep up as Molly bolted down the street. The officer returned to his patrol car and tried to find her, but she was nowhere to be seen. He knew he was going to get in trouble for letting the dog get loose, even if it truly wasn't his fault.

He called to let his supervisor know what happened and hoped he would call the FBI and explain to the Murphy's. No such luck. His supervisor told him continue the search and if she wasn't found soon to return to the Murphy's and tell them himself. He better pray the dog didn't end up under the tires of some vehicle.

Searching for another thirty minutes, the officer finally gave up. He went back to the Murphy's and taking a deep breath, went in. Mr. Murphy was talking with Special Agent McGill in the dining room where all the equipment was set up. He didn't see Mrs. Murphy. He waited until the two men were finished before approaching.

"Mr. Murphy, I'm Officer Pantella, I'm the one who took your dog to the veterinarian, I have to tell you—

"Thank you, so much," Mr. Murphy stated, holding his hand out to the officer. "That was very kind of you. I'm so glad she is going to be okay. She looks good."

"Yes sir," Officer Pantella stated, shaking his hand, but not looking him in the eye. "The vet did say she was fine and…wait, did you say she looks good?" He said, looking up at the man.

"I'm glad the vet gave her a bath. I'd hate for my wife to

see the blood in her coat. That would be unsettling even knowing it wasn't Cautions."

"When did you see your dog?" The officer asked.

"She came running in the door just a few minutes ago and ran straight up to Caution's bedroom and then ran all over the house looking for her. I think she went out to the back yard. Probably needed to do her business as well. Thank you again for bringing her home."

"My pleasure, sir," the officer seemed to stammer.

Molly was indeed in the back yard. She was searching for her favorite person, but she wasn't there. What was there, was Caution's scent as well as the scent of the two mean men. Molly let her lips recess and her teeth show. A faint growl was in her throat. She wanted to get a piece of both of the men. The scent of blood from the man Molly bit was still strong in the grass, although not so much in the air.

Molly sniffed around, getting the scents embedded in her mind. She followed them around the house and back to the front driveway. Here the scents became very faint, but they were still there, all three of them.

Molly went back to the front door which was opened by an attending FBI agent. She was let inside the house and soon found Father. She went around in circles in front of him and sat looking up. He patted her on the head. She again went around in front of him and looked up. She barked once.

"I know," Sean said, "I miss her too. We're looking for her and we'll bring her home soon. I know she misses you too. Now, go lie down, I know you've been through a lot yourself. Go lie down, girl."

She seemed to understand and slowly left out of the room. Obediently, she went to her bed, circled within it a few times, and laid down. With her head down on the bed between her front legs, a slight whine came from deep within the poor, inconsolable dog. Her sad eyes focused mostly on the entrance, hoping Caution would walk in and then run to her side.

Molly's ears perked up just before the front door opened. She sat up with her tail wagging furiously and her head cocked to one side. An FBI agent was in the doorway carrying a large box. He barely took a step inside before he seemed to trip on an invisible barrier. As he lay there stunned for just a second, Molly knew what she needed to do. She bolted for the open door, leaping over the prone agent, and made it outside before he could recover. The door then seemed to close on its own.

Somehow, she knew Caution was not coming home without some help. She ran down the driveway to the open gate, past the FBI agent stationed there and found the familiar scents again. She needed to find her person. She could tell the direction the faint scents led. She knew Caution was in that direction. She knew Caution needed her. She followed her nose.

CHAPTER 29

When the doors were closed once again, Lieutenant Anderson turned back to his witness. "I have just a few more questions, sir."

"Your honor," Lieutenant Harris stood. "With the distraction, I didn't get to object to the witnesses last statement."

"Which one would that be, lieutenant?" The major asked.

"The witnesses' statement about the equipment owned by the killer of his partner."

"I don't see a problem. It seems fine to me," the major stated.

"It's not about the equipment your honor, but the fact the witness made an inflammatory statement that the defendant was the killer of his partner."

"I see what you are saying, Lieutenant Harris, however, even by the defendant's own words, he shot and killed Buckskin Bob. I don't think that's in question. Therefore, Mr. Murphy is the killer of Bob. It's the motive behind the killing which is in question."

"So, your honor," Lieutenant Harris began, turning towards the jury, "the presumption of innocence is still in the defendant's favor and guilt has not been established. There is no witness to show that Mr. Murphy held any grudge, no ill feelings, no reason to shoot a man in cold blood unless the man was doing something which would make Mr. Murphy shoot him."

"Are you giving your final arguments, Lieutenant Harris or are you still questioning this witness?" The major asked. "If so, please continue, with questions, that is."

Lieutenant Harris turned to Carpenter. "Can you tell me your partner's name?"

"The trader laughed. "Of course, it's Buckskin Bob."

"No," Lieutenant Harris stated, "His real name, his given name."

"Well, it's what we've always called him. It's the only name I've known him by."

"So, he's been your partner for five years and you don't even know his real name? Is it even Bob?"

"I don't know."

"How many fights have you been in with him?"

"A few. You know how it is, we're partners We get into a few arguments and sometimes we might have a little too much to drink and get a little rowdy, but nothing serious."

"Does he drink a lot?"

"Sometimes."

"Has he ever drawn a gun or a knife on you?

Carpenter started squirming in the chair. He didn't

answer right away.

"Don't forget you put your hand on a bible and promised to tell the truth," Lieutenant Harris reminded him.

"Not for real, I mean, he never shot me or cut me. He gets a little high strung sometimes."

"Have you ever caught him stealing from you?"

"Well, I wouldn't call it stealing. He was a partner in the business after all."

"Did he ever take anything from a traveler."

"Only what was owed to him."

"How was what he took owed to him?"

"Well, what I mean is sometimes a trade wasn't quite as fair as it might seem and there needed to be more given by one side when they didn't want to give it, so Bob would take it. It was only fair."

"Did it sometimes include horses?"

Again, Carpenter squirmed around in his seat. He knew he said more than he should.

"I'll ask again, Mr. Carpenter, did it include horses?"

"Maybe."

Lieutenant Harris went back to the table and sat down. He whispered with Patrick for a few seconds.

"Lieutenant, do you have anything further from this witness?" The major asked.

There was silence as the lieutenant continued to whisper

with Patrick.

"Lieutenant?"

"Lieutenant Harris?" The major asked impatiently. "Lieut…

"I'm done with this witness, your honor," Lieutenant Harris turned and stated in frustration.

"Lieutenant Anderson, do you have anything further?"

"No, your honor, the prosecution rests its case."

Lieutenant Harris, do you have anything further?"

"I'd like to make my closing statement if you don't mind, your honor. It's short."

"If there are no objections."

There was nothing from the other table.

"Go ahead, lieutenant."

Standing and looking at the jury, the young officer cleared his throat and began. "You've heard here today that Mr. Murphy shot and killed Buckskin Bob. That is the truth. You've also heard he fired one shot, killing Bob instantly. That is the truth. There were no witnesses to this shooting or to anything which would have provoked Mr. Murphy into shooting Bob. That too is the truth. He didn't try to run or hide. He didn't attempt to deny it. So, why did Mr. Murphy shoot Bob? The only truth we can have, told by the only living witness, is that Bob was trying to steal Mr. Murphy's horse and while doing so, attempted to draw a pistol on him. That gave Mr. Murphy the right to defend himself from an armed horse thief who would have shot him if he did not act first. Mr. Murphy only did what any of us would have done and what is allowed by law. He should not be found guilty of anything. Thank you."

"Thank you, Lieutenant Harris, is that all?"

"Your honor, I think I've made our case pretty clear, The defense—

Just then, Big Mike came barreling through the doors and hurried to the table where Lieutenant Harris was standing, He cupped his hand and whispered in his ear. Harris pulled back and looked at Mike as though he were out of his mind. Then Mike started whispering in his ear again.

"All this whispering is not going to get this case finished any sooner. If you have something, please present it, lieutenant, otherwise, I'm ready to give this case to the jury."

"Your honor, if you please, we have one more very important witness to call."

CHAPTER 30

Sam couldn't tell his mom. *Just what would he tell her, anyway?* He wondered. *And just what did the message mean? Was Caution lost? Was she hurt?* He didn't have a phone number to call her.

"Grandpa Bill," Sam exclaimed to himself almost too loud. "I'll call Grandpa Bill; he'll know what to do."

After getting dressed, Sam went to the kitchen, grabbed the phone, and called his grandpa's number. After the fourth ring, he got the recording his grandpa made. *Maybe he's still in bed*, he thought. He didn't leave a message, he needed to do something right then.

He wrote a note for his mother telling her he went out. She would have worried if she got up and he wasn't there. Sam got his backpack out of the closet and took his school stuff out. He went to his savings jar and took a wad of bills out of it, stuffing them into his pocket and dumped the coins into the backpack. Going into the kitchen, he put the note on the refrigerator under a magnet where they kept notes about chores and requests for dinner.

He then got a couple of toaster pastries out of the pantry and grabbed a few bottles of water from the fridge. He gave a push to the fridge door to close it as he turned and headed for the door. What Sam didn't see when the door on the fridge slammed shut, was the magnet fall and the note slip out, floating to the floor. When Sam opened the kitchen door, a rush of air assisted the note to find its way under the fridge.

He left out the side door and unlocked his bicycle and got it out from the carport. He stopped for a second looking around. He wasn't even sure where to begin. He didn't think this out too far; where to look or where to start. He thought for a second and then it hit him. Where else would he look to find Caution? Start at Caution's house. He wasn't sure exactly where it was, but he might know the neighborhood area if he saw it again. It was too far for him to ride his bicycle all the way, so he headed for the closest MARTA train station.

CHAPTER 31

Mike headed to the main doors of the room once more and went outside, he was gone for just a few seconds when the doors flew open and Mike walked back in. This time, Midnight was being led right behind him into the room.

"Your honor, we call Midnight as our next witness." Lieutenant Harris called.

The make-shift courtroom erupted into all kinds of exclamations. Some on the jury couldn't believe their eyes while others laughed at the incredible sight.

Lieutenant Anderson bolted out of his seat, turned, and stared at the spectacle.

"Are you out of your ever-loving mind, lieutenant?" The major exclaimed. "Get that animal out of my building."

"Yes, sir. Just as soon as I get the testimony I need. He is a witness in this case."

"Settle down! The major ordered. "At ease," he finally yelled, giving the military command they would be more familiar with.

Things were now quiet enough to proceed.

"Would you mind explaining yourself, Lieutenant Harris, and I may be using that rank of yours for the last time."

"Yes, sir. I think it may be easier if I ask Mr. Michael O'Brien, the traveling companion of Mr. Murphy to explain. He has information for the court which should be heard. It involves the horse."

"Orderly Sergeant, swear him in. Mr. O'Brien, that is, not the horse," the major said, shaking his head. There was more laughter.

"Your honor," Lieutenant Anderson began.

"I'm going to stop you right there, lieutenant. I've never seen or heard of a horse used as a witness and I want to see this through. Oh, and don't worry, if this goes bad, it will be on Lieutenant Harris, or rather, Private Harris."

"I understand, sir," Lieutenant Harris stated to the major, as he swallowed hard. Turning to Mike, he stated in a low voice, "I hope you know what you're doing."

"Me too," answered Mike.

"Go ahead young man, Let's hear what you have to say, unless you're going to let the horse go first."

"Yes, sir, I mean, no, sir," Mike stammered. "I'm going to tell you, but first, I want to say how sorry I am about your partner, Mr. Carpenter."

Carpenter just gave a nod to Mike.

"That night, when Patrick shot your partner, our horse got spooked and ran off. It didn't take us too long to find her. I'm not sure what's going to happen to my mate, Patrick, but I hope you don't take our horse. If by some miracle of Saint Paddy, I get to keep him, I don't want to take your bridle. We already have one she's used to."

Mike reached up and removed the bridle on Midnight, replacing it with another. "I hope I'm not making a mistake. I know they cost good money," Mike said, handing the bridle to Carpenter. "This is your new bridle from the trading post lot isn't it?"

"Yes, that's one of our bridles, thank you, and no offense to you, but I still think I am owed compensation for my loss."

"Mr. Carpenter," Lieutenant Harris began, "What do you charge for a new bridle and reins set?"

"The set is five dollars."

"How many sets did you sell to the travelers in the wagon train Mr. Murphy was a member of?"

"I don't think we sold any bridles to them on this trip."

"You didn't sell one to Mr. Murphy or to this young man?"

"No, I'd remember that."

"Mr. Carpenter, how did the bridle from your inventory at the trading post end up on Mr. Murphy's horse, Midnight when they already possessed one in good working order and took it off the horse and the horse was hobbled for the night as they did every night?"

"Wait, what? I don't understand. I think you're trying to

confuse me."

"Isn't it possible Buckskin Bob brought the new bridle with him from the trading post to put on the horse before he was going to lead it from the wagon train?"

All eyes were on the trader in the quiet room, waiting for him to give an answer. It never came.

With arguments over, the major turned the case over to the jury, however, the jury didn't even leave the room for deliberation. They just gathered and talked for a minute before advising the major they were ready to announce the verdict.

A folded paper was passed from the jury foreman to the Orderly Sergeant who in turn handed it to the major.

"The accused will stand," the Orderly Sergeant ordered. Patrick Murphy and Lieutenant Harris stood to receive the verdict.

If Patrick was found to be guilty of the murder of Buckskin Bob, he would immediately be marched out of the building to the waiting gallows and hung. No reprieve, no fanfare, no appeals, and no goodbyes. Just outside the fort, a grave was dug in the hard dirt in anticipation of the verdict; the same verdict that always came back.

The major looked at the paper for what seemed an eternity as Patrick's knees began to wobble. The major then looked back at the jury. "Is this verdict each of you has agreed upon from the evidence presented?"

Every member of the jury nodded their heads.

"Then this court has no other option but to accept this verdict."

Patrick's heart was pounding so hard, he didn't think they would ever get the chance to put a rope around his neck before it burst from his chest onto the plankboard floor and cease its beating right there. He let out a heavy sigh, hung his head, and, held his breath ready to hear the death sentence he knew was coming.

The major looked at the young lad, almost sorry he was stretching this out. Almost. "The jury finds you—," the major hesitated for what seemed an eternity, "—not guilty of murdering Buckskin Bob."

There was an immediate shout of disapproval from Carpenter. "What? That's not right."

"Furthermore," the major continued, "the jury finds the horse, Midnight, is rightfully your horse, Mr. Murphy"

Patrick fell into his chair. Lieutenant Harris gave a huge sigh and a slap on Patrick's shoulder.

"Get those shackles off the lad, now," the Orderly Sergeant ordered to one of the soldiers acting as a guard.

Trader Carpenter left the fort an angry and unhappy man. The only thing to show for his loss was now a used bridle.

Mike and Patrick shook hands with Lieutenant Harris and left out the main doors, arm in arm, with Midnight being led right behind them.

The wagon master wasn't too far behind. He also garnered a big smile on his face. The wagon train would be leaving right on time the next morning with the two young Irishmen as part of its company once again.

CHAPTER 32

Bill pulled into the driveway of his daughter's house, right behind the police car. He and Vickie went right in the front door with Bill yelling for his daughter.

"We're in the kitchen, Dad." She was sitting at the small kitchen table with a patrol officer who was taking notes. As soon as she saw him, she went to him and put her head on his chest. "Do you think he's okay? Where would he go?"

"I'm sure he's fine. Tell me what happened." Bill said.

"I got up and came into the kitchen and started to fix breakfast. I went to Sam's room to see what he wanted, and he didn't answer the knock on his door. He thinks he's grown and wants his privacy; you know. I opened the door and saw his bed wasn't made yet, but he wasn't anywhere to be found. He wasn't in the bathroom or outside. The side door was unlocked, but he sometimes forgets to lock it. That's when I called you."

"I'm sorry I missed your first call. I was sleeping hard."

"I only called once."

"You only called once? I bet the earlier call was Sam, but he didn't leave a message. Was anything disturbed? Anything, anywhere?"

"There was a refrigerator magnet on the kitchen floor. I

picked it up and put it back on the fridge.

Bill looked at the fridge. Do you leave notes there?"

"Yes, but there wasn't one."

Bill went over to the unit and looked around. He got down on his knees and looked closer. "Jenny, hand me a fork."

Bill's daughter went to a drawer and retrieved a dinner fork and handed it to him.

Bill used the fork as a rake, attempting to recover something under the fridge. At last, he got a sheet of paper out far enough for him to grab. It was a note from Sam.

"Is his bicycle here?" Her father asked.

"His bicycle? I don't know. I didn't think to look."

Bill went out to the carport and looked. "It's not there."

Bill handed the note to Jenny.

She read it, turning red "He is so grounded," she stated, but also with a sigh of relief.

"Let's wait until we get him home," he said. "Vickie, call McGill and tell him we're still looking for him, but it seems he left on his own."

"Thank God, happy to," Vickie said.

"Oh, hi Vickie," Jenny said. "Sorry about my manners."

"Don't worry about it. Your mind was on Sam and I don't blame you. I'm just glad it wasn't something really bad."

"Vickie, would you move my car for the officer to get out. No need to keep him tied up."

"Thanks, Detective Warner," the officer said. "Is there any word about the little girl who was kidnapped?"

Jenny looked at the officer and then at her father with a face holding a lot of questions. "Dad?"

"No. Nothing yet," Bill said to the officer. He was hoping she and Sam wouldn't find out about the kidnapping until he was able to tell them himself. Now it was out.

"Still keep an eye out for Sam if you don't mind," he told the officer. "We still need to get him home."

"Sure thing," the officer stated, putting his notebook away. "I'll call you if there's any word."

"Thanks," Bill said.

"Yes, thank you, so much," Jenny said.

After the officer went out the door and before Vickie came back in, Jenny gave a hard look at her father. "What's this about a little girl being kidnapped? Is it the same little girl who Sam met the other day?"

"Well, yes, but Sam has nothing to do with it. I don't even think he knows about it yet. It just happened yesterday, and I didn't tell him."

"Well, it looks like he knows something. He's never acted this way before. Not since he found that stupid coin and playing policeman with you. Maybe it's cursed."

"Maybe it is," he said, not going into any further detail.

Vickie came back in and tossed the keys to Bill. "What's

the plan?"

"How about finding your grandson and bringing him home safe and sound," Jenny stated, hands on her hips.

"That's just exactly what we are going to do, sweetheart" Bill said.

"And I'm going to make sure he does," Vickie chimed in.

"Good." What are you doing standing here then? Go," Jenny said. "I want my son home."

"We all do," Bill said.

Bill and Vickie got out to his car and pulled out.

"Where do you think he could have gone?" Vickie asked.

"There's only one place I can think of if he wants to help Caution," Bill said.

"The only place he has ever seen her, at her house," Vickie said.

"Exactly," Bill said.

"He's on a bicycle. He couldn't have gone very far, it's a long way."

"He's very resourceful," Bill said. "He'll find a way. He won't give up."

"Not if he's anything like you. What about a bus or train?" Vickie suggested.

"Exactly what I was thinking. I don't know how much he paid attention to my driving us over there. He may have a general idea where her house is, but he might need some help."

"I'll call MARTA Police and see if they can monitor their train stations between here and there as well as their bus routes. A ten-year-old boy with a bicycle should be easy to spot. We might get lucky," Vickie stated.

"I pray we do. Thanks, partner," Bill said, forcing a slight smile through his worried face.

William N. Gilmore

CHAPTER 33

Right after the full partnership meeting and now armed with all the information and maps as well as funding provided by Mr. Murphy, John Gray headed for Savannah. Once there, he leased a trawler. He quickly outfitted it with the most modern equipment for deep ocean searches including side-scanning sonar, underwater metal detectors, camera mounted submersibles and ROV's, and magnetometers. He was also counting on an old contact who possessed a one-man, deep-submersible vehicle if the need arose. But first, he needed to find the right shipwreck.

Upon learning about the kidnapping, John wanted to return and help find Caution, or at least be of some help there to the Murphy's during this time, however, he was tasked by Sean Murphy to go ahead with the plans to search and locate the shipwreck and the treasure without him. He told John the demands of the kidnapper, how little time there was, and how important it was for him to succeed; for Caution.

John knew he wouldn't be able to take all this on alone and needed someone who was experienced, available, and above all, someone whom he could trust. That combo was a tricky thing to find in the treasure hunting world.

Mr. Murphy insisted there should be a new security team

to accompany John, but instead, Tommy McGill requisitioned two FBI agents with special diving qualification, just in case, to be part of John's crew, meeting him up the coast.

Trying to keep the nature of the expedition secret was going to be a challenge at best. What information the kidnappers possessed was unclear and there was bound to be someone watching John's movements and reporting back to them.

The ship John leased was out of his home port of Savannah for security reasons. It would take several days to get to the northeast coastal area to even think about starting their search. Although time was a factor, John needed to be mindful of the weather and water conditions in the search area during this time of year.

There would be no special permits or notifications to any state or federal government about their search and hopeful recovery. If anyone inquired about what they were doing, it would be explained as an underwater nature photography and film documentary expedition sponsored by a world-class magazine. Something John was also known for and was hired to do in the past. If anyone could find the shipwrecks, John was the one to bet on.

John was securing equipment on the deck of the boat when he noticed one of his FBI security team pull out a semi-automatic pistol and cover it with a towel as he moved in front of John. He and his partner were now on high alert.

"Ahoy," came a familiar voice from the dock.

"It's okay, George," John said to the agent. "It's a friend."

John moved over to the gunwale of the boat and called out over the side. "Ahoy, yourself," he laughed.

"Permission to come aboard?"

"You're late. I expected you yesterday."

"Well, you didn't give me much notice. I needed to find someone to take care of my dog."

"You still have the old mutt?"

"No. She's crossed the rainbow bridge. I have a new pup now."

"Sorry about the old girl. I knew she meant a lot to you."

"Are you going to make me stand down here all day or are you going to help me get my equipment on board?"

John hurried down the ship's gangplank to the dock and went and gave her a big hug. "It's good to see you, Kelly. I've missed you."

"That's your fault. You don't call, you don't write. You *can* write, can't you? You didn't let a moray eel bite off your fingers, did you?" She asked with a laugh, taking his hands. "Nope, still there."

"I called," John protested weakly, pulling his hands back. "That's why you're here."

"Oh, so, you call, and I'm supposed to drop everything

and come running. Maybe I should think twice about this. Maybe I should—

"Kelly, I need you," John said.

Kelly looked at him. Something in his face showed real concern. His voice was different, more serious.

"I really need you on this," John repeated, looking straight into her eyes with a hint of desperation.

"You were very vague about this trip, John, what's going on?" She asked as she noticed the men on the boat watching them. "Who's your crew? They seem very intense."

"I guess I better tell you everything before we get your stuff on the boat. You may change your mind about helping me."

"John, are you in trouble?"

"It's not me. It's a close friend and possibly, the life of a sweet and innocent little girl."

It was Kelly's time to give John a strange look.

"Oh, no. No. Not mine," John insisted. "The people I work for. It's their daughter."

"Let's go ahead and get the stuff on the boat. You know I'd never refuse to help you, no matter what it was."

Onboard the boat, John told Kelly everything. They worked together on many dives, saving each other's lives several times over. She was one of a handful of people he could trust with the information and thought it only right for her to know the dangers before signing up for this adventure.

"Who else do you have besides your two hunky FBI friends?" Kelly asked.

"Barnes is meeting us in Virginia Beach."

"Barnes?" Kelly questioned. "Why Barnes? He's a drunk. He almost got you killed. Have you forgotten about that? He sent you down with the wrong tanks and you got the bends. You were in the hospital for three days."

"It wasn't intentional. He made a stupid mistake."

"Mistakes like that we don't need," Kelly insisted.

"That was five years ago. He's clean now, has been for years. I'd rather have him than someone I don't know and can't be sure if they can be trusted."

"I'm not sure I can work with him," Kelly stated.

"It was my life that day and I got over it. I need you to get over it too. I need you. I need you both, and besides, there is no one else to get with this short amount of time."

"Fine," she said sarcastically, "just keep him away from me," Kelly insisted. "I'll check my own tanks and equipment."

"Fine by me. Let's get underway."

CHAPTER 34

Sam got to the MARTA train station where he asked a man where he could buy a ticket. He was shown an automated ticket dispenser where he purchased a ticket. He made his way to the entry gate where he put his ticket into a machine that grabbed the ticket at one end and spit it out at the other. He took his ticket and made his way along the platform where there was a large map of the train routes.

He wasn't sure which train to take. just that Caution's house was north of the city in an area called Buckhead. He heard of the area before but couldn't ever remember being there before meeting Caution. He recalled the general area where Caution lived, but not the street names or the house number. He pushed his brain to try and remember what the house looked like.

Sam found on the map the route the train took north with a stop in Buckhead. He pushed his bike to the end of the platform to wait for the next train. After about seven minutes, he saw a train coming down the tracks. It wasn't a train in the true sense of the word as he remembered trains. It was a square, blunt-nosed, silver thing with lots of windows. He saw them before but was never on one nor even this close.

When the train came to a stop, doors on each car slid

open with a "whoosh". There were not too many people in this car but the ones who were, looked at the young boy as he pushed his bike into the compartment and to the end of the car where he sat down.

Sam looked around at the inside of the train car, seeing advertisements and a colored route map overhead. He was startled by the doors closing on the train and the sudden jump of acceleration. It was like the start of one of the rollercoaster rides at Six Flags. He doubted it would go upside down or into a corkscrew, but he hoped there wouldn't be any steep hills or drop-offs. He held a little tighter onto his bike.

Sam looked out the window as the train sped along, staring at the sights going by. He saw the train was traveling parallel to a road he thought he remembered which gave him a little more confidence he was going in the right direction.

The train suddenly seemed to decelerate and he almost lost control of his bicycle as it rolled forward a bit. The train came to a stop and the doors swooshed opened again at another station. This was not the place he wanted to get off. Not yet. As the doors closed, he braced for the movement of the car. He was quickly becoming accustomed to how the train worked. He smiled.

There were many more stops before he would be where he needed to start looking for Caution's neighborhood. He was sure he would recognize it. Not all the houses and yards looked the same as they did in his mom's area. In fact, Caution's house and yard took up most of a whole neighborhood all by itself.

Sam hadn't thought about it and he wasn't sure what he would say when he got there. He didn't want them to think he was crazy. What if Caution wasn't there? What if no one was home? What kind of help did she need that her parents couldn't do something about? What could he do? One thing for sure, unless he didn't have a choice, he wasn't going to tell anyone about the dream or the mirror.

CHAPTER 35

"Did you find Olson?" Dearing asked.

"No," Kline answered almost in disgust as she rubbed the area around her wrists where the handcuffs left marks. "And that stupid private eye didn't know where he was either, or at least that's what he said before I shot him. Is Olson all that important?"

"To me he is. And don't forget, I need *him* alive."

"Sure thing, uncle. If he lets me."

"Did you learn anything from the cops?"

"Those two who found me in Olson's office think you have something to do with all of this, but they don't know what. They don't know what Olson knows or where he is either. And they're not both cops, at least, not the guy anymore. He's retired. The detective, her name is Winston, she's the one who shot Uncle Adam."

Dearing almost swerved off the road. "Son of a...," he growled angerly, hitting the flat of his fist against the steering wheel. "I knew it must have been one of them."

"He was there when she shot him. We'll make them both pay," she promised.

"We'll get to them soon enough. I've got another job for

you first."

*

Caution woke to aching muscles all over. There was no way to tell what time it was or even if it was day or night. She tried to stretch the best she could, but with the new tape around her wrists and ankles as she sat in the small space of the box, the top just barely open, it just wouldn't work.

She listened through the hood and the box to see if she could hear Roger or Quin and she heard two distinct sounds of snoring. One seemed farther away. Both appeared to be sleeping, but she couldn't tell which snore belonged to which man. One would snore and then the other seemed to answer with his own snore, like frogs calling to each other in the night.

She desperately needed to go to the bathroom, but she didn't dare wake either man. Doing so would surely make them mad and she didn't want that. Instead, to take her mind off her needs, she went over all the information she was gathering about the two men, her location, and the thoughts of what Vickie and her grandpa would do.

Her grandpa said he was once a prisoner himself; she wondered what he meant by that. Where? When? And why?

She heard the tune that told her Roger's telephone was going off and the snoring of the man closest to her stopped.

"Hello," Roger's voice said. "No, no problems with the girl. Quin was forced to abandon the rental van last night. Some kind of mechanical problem, but I instructed him wipe it all down, inside and out before leaving it. We need some kind of transportation to replace it."

There was silence for a few minutes, and she didn't hear Quin's snoring anymore.

"How long is it going to be?" Roger asked, sounding perturbed, apparently to the person on the other end of the phone, possibly their boss. "Yes, sir," Roger said, continuing the conversation. "I understand. We're going to need some things then, most importantly, a means of transportation for supply runs or just in case we need to bug out to another location in a hurry. We need some cash, food, water, and Quin needs some medical stuff to treat his dog bite."

Caution could hear Quin from farther away asking, "What's he saying?"

"Shut up," Roger must have said to Quin in a quieter voice, then returning to his normal voice, "Yes, sir, if that's what needs to be done, you can count on us to do it. It won't be a problem."

Caution was afraid they were talking about her. She was sure they were, and it didn't sound good.

CHAPTER 36

The train came to a stop at one of the stations Sam was sure was the closest one to where he would find Caution's house. He knew there was still a long way to go and was glad he brought his bike. This could take a while. Many of the large houses were behind big gates and sometimes, you couldn't see the house at all. He was sure he'd remember it if he saw it.

Sam continued to ride around the neighborhoods trying to remember the drive his grandpa made, but nothing looked familiar. He didn't pay enough attention. At one point, he thought he saw a dog like Caution's several blocks up, but her dog wouldn't be out in the streets.

He saw a woman walking a small dog up ahead and pulled over to the side of the road. As she approached, the dog began to bark at him.

"Excuse me, ma'am. Would you happen to know which house the Murphy's live in?"

"No, I'm afraid not," she said, over the barking and growling while holding her little dog back from attacking Sam's bicycle. "I'm new to the area."

"Okay, thank you, anyway," Sam said. He pushed off from the curb to another round of barks and growls as the small dog tugged at its leash to get to the ferocious and menacing bicycle, finally returning to its owners' side, proud of defeating and chasing off the strange creature.

Sam rode around the area for about an hour without any luck when he stopped and took one of the bottles of water from his backpack. The day was already warm, and he was starting to sweat. His hold on the bike's rubber grips was slippery even after rubbing his hands on his pants several times. Along with his exhaustion, he was starting to get frustrated and afraid he wouldn't be able to find the house.

Suddenly, he saw something which might help. Just down the street was a mail truck, stopping and putting mail in the boxes of the houses on his side of the street. He put the water bottle back into his backpack and took off for one of the boxes on the truck's route. Sam was straddling his bike next to a brick mailbox when the truck pulled up.

"Hey there, young man. Getting hot enough for you?" the man in the short sleeve, blue shirt and blue-grey shorts asked.

"Yes sir, it is," Sam returned. "I'm trying to find the home of the Murphy's and their daughter, Caution. Would you know which house it is?"

"You mean the little girl who's missing?" the postal worker asked. "It's six blocks over," he said, pointing in the direction, "but I wouldn't go over there right now, they've got all those FBI guys running around there. Are you a friend of hers?"

"Missing?" Sam exclaimed. "FBI?"

The mail carrier now felt uncomfortable. "I'm sorry, I thought you knew, being a friend of hers. I'm sure they'll find her soon and the people who took her."

Sam barely heard the last part of what the mailman was saying as he took off in the direction where the Murphy house was located. Sam stood, pushing the peddles as fast as his legs would allow him, making the distance of the six-block trek in record time, disregarding his exhaustion and the heat.

Sam saw the big gate and recognized Caution's house down the long driveway. There was a man in a blue vest-jacket standing at the gate just outside a big, black SUV. As Sam got closer, he saw the yellow FBI on the vest. He headed straight for him.

The FBI agent noticed the young man on the bicycle but didn't expect him to come right at the partially opened gate.

"Whoa there, cowboy," the agent said as he blocked the way with his body. "Where do you think you're going?"

As Sam came to a sliding stop just feet from the agent, he said, "I've got to see Mr. Murphy."

"Oh, do you now?" the agent returned. "I guess you have an appointment?"

"No, but it's really important."

"Well, he's an important person and he's very busy right now," the agent said, trying to wave the kid off. He didn't have time for this.

"I'm a friend of Caution's and she's in trouble," Sam said, trying to reason with the agent.

"What do you know about the little girl?" the agent asked, now a little more intrigued.

Sam laid down his bicycle right at the gate and then tried to get past the agent, but he was too quick, grabbing Sam by the arm.

Just then, a car pulled up to the gate and two people got out. The driver yelled at the agent to let the boy go and he didn't say it nicely.

"Grandpa Bill," Sam yelled, yanking loose from the surprised agent's grip.

"What's going on here, agent?" Vickie demanded.

Stammering at first, the agent told them what occurred. "This young man, I'm sorry, I didn't know he was your grandson, he just tried to get past me to get to the house. I stopped him. He said the little girl was in trouble. I didn't have time to find out what he meant or what he knows."

"Sam, please go have a seat in my car."

"But Grandpa Bill, I need to tell you—"

"And you will, Sam. Give me just a minute, please.

"I'll go with you," Vickie said, taking Sam's hand and guiding him to the car.

Sam turned back towards the gate, "My bicycle," he said.

"We'll take care of it," Bill said, giving Sam a wink.

Vickie opened the back-passenger side door for Sam, closing it after he got in then got into the front seat, keeping an eye on Bill.

"What's grandpa saying to the FBI agent?" Sam asked, scooting up to the space between the two front seats.

"Oh, I'm sure he's just thanking him for all the dedicated work they're doing," Vickie said, trying not to give away the knowing smile she showed on her face.

After a few minutes, Bill left the agent and took Sam's bicycle to the rear of his car and placed it in the trunk, securing it with bunji cords he stored there. The FBI agent, a forced smile on his red face, opened the gate all the way for them to drive up to the house. He gave a friendly wave to Sam as he went by.

CHAPTER 37

The boys were happy to get back on the trail, leaving Fort Laramie in their dust. They thought Midnight might be happy to leave too.

"I'm really glad you didn't get hung," Mike said to Patrick after nothing was said about the incident for several hours.

"Not as bloody glad as I am," Patrick said. "That was smart bringing in Midnight with the bridle Buckskin Bob put on him."

"Well, that's not exactly how it was," Mike confessed. "Buckskin Bob didn't put the new bridle on Midnight."

"What are you talking about? Of course, he did. It's the one Midnight was wearing when you brought him into the courtroom."

"It's the one he was wearing because I put it on him."

"Bloody hell," Patrick exclaimed.

"I bought the new bridle from Buckskin Bob earlier. It was going to be a surprise gift for you to put on Midnight yourself. No one else knew. The bridle he put on Midnight while trying to steal him was the one I took off him and left hanging from the wagon."

"You lied in court," Patrick accused Mike in horror, "to the judge and the jury after you swore."

"Oh, no I didn't," Mike declared. "No one ever asked me if I bought a bridle. I just said if I got to keep Midnight, I didn't want their new bridle. And that's the bloody truth. I wouldn't want nothin' from none of them."

"But you didn't tell them you bought the bridle from Buckskin Bob or that it was you who put it on Midnight," Patrick tried to reason.

"No one bothered to ask me, so it wasn't no lie. Besides, it helped save your sorry, Irish soul. You shot him in self-defense, or he would have shot you and that would have been the real murder. Why should you hang for staying alive?"

"You took a big risk, you eejit."

"Not me," Mike claimed," I didn't have nothin' to lose but my partner and my best friend. I figured if they hung you I would just go find another."

"And just where would you be finding a better partner and friend? Who would it be staking you for you to get rich and build your marvelous castle you have your heart set on? Better not to chance it."

"The ghost of Patrick Murphy would be staking me. The chest is still in the wagon and you wouldn't be having any need for it, dangling from the new rope they promised you."

"Well, you have a point there now, don't you, but you

better know, I be coming back to haunt you the rest of your days, Michael Shannon Andrew O'Brien."

They both enjoyed a strained laugh over all of this, but Mike still preserved an unanswered question on his mind he knew he couldn't ask. *What's it like to kill a man?*

CHAPTER 38

"Grandpa Bill, Caution's in trouble," Sam exclaimed as they continued up the drive to the house.

"Yes, Sam, we know. We're trying to find her," Bill said.

"Did she get lost?" Sam asked, not fully grasping the situation.

"No, Sam," Vickie said, turning in her seat to face him. "I hate to tell you," she began with a sad look on her face, "but some bad men came to her house and took her away. She was kidnapped. We don't know where she is. How did you know she was in trouble?"

Here it was. How was he going to explain what happened to him at his house? What could he say that didn't make him look like a little kid with a wild imagination or a crazy person? He hadn't thought up an answer to that yet.

"I just knew," Sam said. "Something was telling me she was in trouble and I needed to help her."

"Well, your instincts were right, Sam," Vickie said. "But I still don't understand what made you go through all the problems to get here."

Sam was about to say something but got a reprieve as they came to a stop at the front entrance of the big house.

"We'll talk more about this later, Sam," Grandpa Bill said. "Let's go inside and see if there's any more news. I've got to call your mom and tell her we found you and you're okay. I don't think she's very happy with you right now."

"But she was still asleep when I left. I even tried to call you before I put a note on the refrigerator so she would find it and not worry," Sam tried to explain.

"I'm sorry I missed your call. Your mom couldn't find a note when she found you gone. She called me in a panic. When we got to your house, I got lucky and found the note. It came loose and fell under the fridge."

"Oh," was all Sam could muster while looking down.

They all exited the car and went into the house. The first thing Bill did was call his daughter. He was right, she was not happy with Sam, not a bit, but she was grateful and relieved he was safe and with his grandpa.

Meanwhile, Vickie went into the makeshift control room and checked in with Agent McGill to see if there were any further developments. She was shocked to learn the girl, whatever her real name might be, from Olson's office, escaped. The two FBI agents escorting her to their office suffered non-life-threatening injuries when their SUV was T-boned. The male agent was admitted to the hospital with a concussion and broken ribs. The female agent, still under observation at the hospital, suffered bumps and bruises, most notably, one right between the eyes where she said she was punched by someone she believed may have been male. She was unable to give any further descriptions or information.

The other vehicle involved in the crash; a large construction truck, was abandoned at the scene. It was reported stolen earlier in the day. There was no useful evidence found in the truck. There were no suspects.

"Dearing's your suspect," Vickie insisted after hearing the report. "He's the mastermind behind everything going on. Bill will tell you. He has to be. Bring him in and I guarantee I'll get him to tell us where Caution is.

Mr. Murphy walked into his converted dining room. "I thought I heard your voice in here," he said to Vickie.

"How are you holding up, Mr. Murphy?" Vickie asked. "How's your wife doing?"

"We're both doing the best we can. Sheila's upstairs laying down trying to get some rest, but I know she's having a challenging time with it. It's the waiting and hoping and waiting some more. Did I hear you say there's a suspect?" Mr. Murphy inquired.

Vickie realized she needed to tread lightly here without giving any false hope. "We're looking at a lot of possibilities, checking things out. It takes a lot of time and resources and we have to be careful we don't tip our hand."

"Didn't you mention the name, Dearing?" Sean asked.

"He's the coin dealer who Bill dealt with and also the name of the guy you shot. It can't be a coincidence. What are you doing about this, Agent McGill?"

"We're looking into it," Tommy said. "We don't have any proof the living Dearing is involved and we're not sure how deep Adam Dearing is, or rather, was involved, if he was working on his own, with his brother, or possibly with someone else."

"Are you going to bring him in for questioning?" Sean asked.

"Not until we get something more on him. If we push too hard, He may cut his ties with Caution. Right now, he thinks he's in charge and we want him to continue believing it."

Mrs. Murphy walked into the dining room and asked if there was any news.

"You should be laying down," Sean said with concern for his wife as he quickly went over and put his arm around her waist; giving her support.

"I'm much better now, physically anyway. I just couldn't sleep. I've got to keep busy, keep my mind off the terrible thoughts I've been having."

"There's no need for terrible thoughts," Mr. Murphy cautioned sympathetically. "Caution will be back home soon, safe and sound," he said, trying to sound believing and reassuring. "We're getting closer to finding her, I promise. Why don't you take Molly out for a walk," he suggested, "she may need to go out and do her business and the fresh air will do you good."

"That's probably a good idea," she said, nodding. She gave Sean a weak smile and walked off calling for Molly.

Bill and Sam walked into the room and Sam walked over to Mr. Murphy.

"I'm sure Caution will be back real soon, sir. There's a lot of really great people looking for her. They'll find her and bring her home safe."

"Thank you, Sam. I'm sure they will." Mr. Murphy's voice began to crack as he finished that last part. He needed to be strong for his wife, and he pretended to have it together, but he needed a little faith himself. Others tried to comfort and reassure him, but it came with a true conviction, so pure, from a boy not much older than his missing daughter.

William N. Gilmore

CHAPTER 39

The sailing was uneventful the whole trip up the Eastern Coast and when they arrived at Virginia Beach, John docked at a prearranged location by a marine gas station for boats. They wouldn't be staying long, just enough to fill up the gas tanks and pick up Barnes.

John hoped he would be on time, at the dock waiting for them, but mostly he prayed he would be sober like he told Kelly. He didn't tell Kelly he hadn't seen or spoken with Barnes in years and he was going just by what he was told by him over the phone. He was taking a big gamble, but if Barnes was clean, he was the best at what he did.

There was no sign of Barnes anywhere on the dock and John tried to hide his frustration and worry. John tied up the boat and he and Kelly with George as their shadow, went to ask around about him, leaving Frank to watch the boat.

There was a bait shop close by and John asked the old man running it if he knew Barnes or if he saw anyone looking like they were waiting on someone.

"I think who you're looking for is up at the bar," he said, pointing with his thumb up to the other end of the dock. "I seen him walking around here for a while like a lost puppy dog."

"Well, of course, that's where he'd be," Kelly said. "Any bets on how long it will take to sober him up?"

John got a sinking feeling in his gut. This was a mistake.

As John and Kelly approached the bar, the door flew open and out walked a big man with long hair, a straggly beard, tattoos covering both arms, a bright-pink tank top with blue shorts, and matching flip-flops. Another thing which stood out about this man was his prosthetic right leg.

"Holy crap," the man blurted out. "You're finally here. It's about friggin' time." He grabbed John in a big bear hug lifting him off the ground a few inches. George started to step forward reaching for his concealed weapon, but Kelly shook her head and just said, "Barnes."

George, wearing a dark set of aviator sunglasses seemed to be looking over the top of them at this wild-looking man with one good leg and relaxed, but only just a bit.

Barnes put John down and looked over at Kelly. He turned to her and held his arms out. Kelly backed up.

"Don't tell me you're still mad at me. I've changed."

Kelly looked over at the bar then back at Barnes. "Yeah, right."

"Oh, no. I just needed to go in to use the head," Barnes said. "I don't touch the stuff anymore. Not for years." He crossed his heart then held his right hand up, palm out. "I swear." Then he opened his mouth and exhaled a breath at Kelly.

She stared at him for a long few seconds and saw his eyes were clear and his hands weren't shaking. "That's good. I'm happy for you," Kelly said with a bit of sarcasm anyway.

"John, help me out here," Barnes begged.

"You know I can't blame her, but I'm trying to look past it. We're giving you this chance. One only, that's it," John said. "If you screw it up, I'll throw you overboard to the sharks myself."

"Sure, it won't be a problem. Who's your friend here?"

"This is George. I'll introduce you properly to everyone when we get on the boat. Where's your gear?"

"In the back of my truck. I parked it across the street. You said you needed me, and you'd tell me what was going on when we met up, so, here we are, what's going on?"

"We're going on a dive," John said. "Are you in or out?"

"Well, that doesn't tell me much." He looked over at George then back to John. He put the blade of his hand up to the other side of his mouth and leaned forward. "Is this a spy mission?" he asked in almost a whisper.

"Ah…no," John said back in his own whisper.

"Am I getting paid?" Barnes asked in his normal voice.

"Yes, but if you delay us any longer, I'm going to start subtracting from it."

"Who gets to sleep with Kelly?"

"What the—?" Kelly said, looking shocked.

"Just kidding," Barnes said laughing, giving John a wink. "We've got a lot to catch up on. I've missed you guys. This is going to be fun."

They got all of Barnes equipment to the boat in one haul and secured it away on the deck. Barnes took one look at Frank and wondered if his first guess wasn't so far off after all.

Barnes was a former Naval Intelligence Officer and SEAL. During an operation in Iraq, he was hit by a sniper's bullet. He didn't think it was bad at first, but the bullet hit bone and fragmented into many pieces. It caused internal damage all up and down his lower leg.

He wasn't getting blood to the lower part of the leg and his leg and foot were now swollen to twice their size, infection set in, and the tissue was dying. Even after numerous operations things never got better. Doctors told him it could not be repaired, and the leg would be useless to him, causing problems the rest of his life. Before the doctor's recommendation and without hesitation, Barnes told them to take it off.

With the advancement in the field of prosthetics at the VA, Barnes was fitted with special devices allowing him not only to live a normal life but to continue his love of sport diving. He even assisted in the development of special prosthetics just for other amputees who for whatever reason, lost one or both legs and wanted to learn or to continue diving. He referred to the new prosthetic legs as 'Snap-on Tools'.

During one outing in the Florida Keys, he chanced upon a meeting with John in a bar, a fellow diver who was impressed with him and his story. They became fast friends and Barnes, who insisted he be called just 'Barnes', helped John on some of his dives. On one of those dives, he met Kelly. She was the old girlfriend of one of John's buddies. The relationship went sour, but John and Kelly remained friends. John taught her how to dive, assisting in getting her trained and certified for all the types of diving she wanted to do.

They were all good friends until Barnes began drinking more and more. He was having flashbacks of his war experiences and getting shot. He started making small mistakes and missing planned outings. He was also becoming more aggressive and verbally abusive. He started several bar fights, getting kicked out or banned from most of the establishments around Virginia Beach.

One day, John and Kelly were waiting on him for a dive. A boat was chartered and time was money. They went to check on him at his flat and found him passed out. They tried to get him up and into the shower, but he resisted, taking a swing at John, hitting Kelly instead.

The friendship was strained, but John talked Kelly into giving him another chance after Barnes remained sober for a couple of weeks and apologized more than once to both of them.

Several days later, on one of the dives John planned for

the three of them, Barnes showed up, obviously having been drinking, but he wasn't staggering or incoherent. Still, John wouldn't let him dive and allowed him man the equipment which was his usual job. Barnes readied a set of tanks for them for their second dive while John and Kelly were under.

On the second, deeper dive, John got into trouble because the air mixture in his tank was wrong and he got a case of the bends. Nitrogen bubbles in his blood. A very painful and potentially deadly situation.

John needed to be rushed back to shore and then to the hospital. He spent several days recovering. Kelly stayed with John the whole time and would not let Barnes visit him, telling him to stay away from them; for good. He did just that until he received the call from John. If he was sober, if he could stay sober, he needed him.

Nearly killing his friend sent a wake-up call to Barnes' brain and heart, and ever since that day, he hadn't touched a drop. Not even a beer. He also started counseling for his PTSD.

John paid for the special marine fuel with a credit card Mr. Murphy supplied him and they shoved off. John didn't want to tell Barnes what was truly going on until they were well out to sea.

The projected weather for the Northeast Coast looked spotty over the next two weeks and John hoped the FBI would find Caution well before any dangerous weather blew in. If not, he knew he would need to find the sunken ship and the treasure it contained in the brief time left.

As the ship and its crew sailed further away, a pair of eyes looking through high-powered binoculars watched their movements from another boat tied up near the same dock.

"Your orders, ma'am?"

Terry Kline lowered the binoculars. "Give them another ten minutes, then go ahead and cast off," she said to the boat's skipper. "And you can bring me another martini."

"Aye, ma'am," he said saluting.

CHAPTER 40

As Patrick and Mike observed while they traveled this new country which they now called their own, many spectacular sights adorned the vast lands they crossed. Some, as they observed, were the more notable rock formations which stood out for one reason or another and were waypoints the wagon trains set as destinations, camping there for two or three nights when there were water and grass for the animals.

One of the more famous of these locations was Independence Rock. In 1830, a fur trapper held a celebration there on July 4, and the granite dome became known as Independence Rock.

Travelers have been carving their names, dates, epigraphs, and messages left for loved ones and for future travelers who followed this route, on the rock for many years.

In 1840, a missionary emigrant, Father Pierre-Jean De Smet put his name on the rock and referred to the location as the *Register of the Desert.*

Another reason for the name was it was hoped by the wagon masters and pioneers to reach Independence Rock by July 4 to beat the first snows and any harsh weather sure to come further ahead in the high mountains in the later months.

When the wagon trains arrived in the area, they camped close to the Sweetwater River. The wagon trains would spend a couple of days along the river to rest, water and feed the animals, as well as explore the area.

The flat top of Independence Rock was a good place to see a 360-degree panoramic site of the area. Sometimes, they would orchestrate dances with music provided by bands from the wagon trains on the top of the mountain.

Hundreds, if not thousands of names were carved or painted on the rock and many took the time to add theirs. Some were even in red and yellow paints.

Patrick and Mike debated about adding their names in the hard granite, but instead, they watched as one of their traveling companions worked hard carving his name and didn't want to exert themselves in the heat. It took him about an hour to put his name and date in the rock, but it is still there to this date; R. McCord-July 4-1850.

Many of the names and dates previously put on the rock were illegible by their arrival and some, especially those put on with chalk or paint were long gone. Even a large cross carved into the rock by John Fremont is gone, but it was blasted away by other emigrants in 1848 believing it was a symbol of the Pope in Rome.

Not far from Independence Rock was the strange formation of Devil's Gate. A natural divide in the mountain carved out by the Sweetwater River eons ago. It was too narrow for wagons, but it still was an interesting sight to see and many left their names on that formation as well.

There were several graves close to the area too. One notable and still easy to read marker was for an F. R. Fulkerson with the date of his death being July 1, 1847. Possibly due to illness.

Patrick and Mike took advantage of the long stop to grease the axles and wheels plus a few other minor repairs and maintenance on the wagon. It was holding up remarkably well on the journey, so far. A testament to the fine workmanship of Hiram Young.

Some of the wagons experienced bent wheels and hubs or broken and cracked axles. Many were lucky they carried replacements or could make repairs on the trail. Too many wagons were abandoned because of breaking down or even being washed away while crossing rivers or getting stuck so deep in muddy suck holes, they couldn't be recovered.

The wagon train was down from the original one hundred to about seventy-five wagons now. Six people died they were aware of, possibly more with the wagons which turned around or split off. A couple of wagons were being kept separated from the rest due to illnesses.

There was sure to be more deaths and fewer wagons before they got to their destinations. The roughest part of the trail so far was just ahead.

.

CHAPTER 41

While Sam and Mr. Murphy were talking, Sheila Murphy came back into the room.

"Sean, I can't find Molly anywhere. She won't come when I call for her."

"Maybe she's outside on the property somewhere. She knows not to run off."

"I think she's looking for Caution. She tried to stop the men who took her, and she knows she's not here. Since she's been back, I've seen her go around the house checking out every room."

"Excuse me," Sam said. "I think I saw Molly when I was trying to find your house. She was several blocks over, running in the street."

"When you were trying to find our house?" Mr. Murphy asked, looking at Bill with a questioning expression.

"Sam didn't know about Caution's abduction, but said he felt something was wrong and left his mom's house on his bicycle to come here," Bill explained.

"You came all this way on your bicycle, young man?" Mr. Murphy asked, surprised.

"No, sir. I rode the train most of the way."

Sean couldn't help but smile a little. "Very impressive. What made you think something was wrong, Sam?"

Sam shuffled his feet around a little and looked down, he didn't say anything intelligible and tugged on the front of his shirt. He seemed to be almost embarrassed or scared to say anything further.

"Sam, Mr. Murphy is asking you a question. Please don't be rude."

"I just had a feeling," Sam mumbled without looking up.

"Mr. Warner; Bill," Sean began, "would you mind if Sam and I talked in private for a few minutes in my study. I'd like to hear more about this, and I think he may feel more comfortable with a one on one conversation."

Bill seemed a little hesitant with the suggestion at first but saw Sean's easy and agreeable look and knew he would be respectful of Sam.

"Sam, would you be willing to speak with Mr. Murphy on your own? You don't have to if you don't want to. It's up to you."

"Okay," Sam said, again without looking up.

"Sam, let's go into my study where we can sit and have a talk." He started to walk in the study's direction with Sam following when Sam turned.

"Don't forget about Molly. She's out in the road looking for Caution and I'd hate for her to get hit by a car."

"Don't worry," Vickie said. "We'll go find her."

"Or maybe, just maybe, we can use her," Bill said, his eyes getting wider and a slight smile came on his face.

"What do you mean?" Mrs. Murphy asked.

"Molly is on Caution's scent. She's tracking her," Bill said excitedly. "She's better than a bloodhound. She has her love for Caution guiding her."

"Vickie, put a BOLO out on Molly but don't have them pick her up. I want to know exactly where she is and in what direction she's headed. Dollars to doughnuts she's headed to the area where the white van was recovered. Caution has got to be somewhere in that area and she just might be able to show us where."

*

Sean opened the door to his study, allowing Sam to enter first.

"Please have a seat, Sam. Can I get you something to drink or snack on?"

"No, sir. Thank you, sir," Sam said timidly as he sat in a large chair facing a big wooden desk. Mr. Murphy sat in the chair behind the desk.

"Sam, you can relax. I won't bite you, or yell, or anything like that. I just want to talk. I want you to trust me. Think of it like you're talking to your Grandpa Bill."

Sam showed a slight grimace on his face.

"Or, like you're talking to Caution," Sean could tell he found the better tactic.

"Sam, you said you experienced a feeling something was wrong; do you mean you thought Caution was in trouble?"

"Yes, sir. Something like that."

"Did she say something to you when you were over here before, on the day you met? Something about being in trouble?"

"Oh, no, sir. We had fun that day. I like her, I mean, she's nice."

Sean gave a smile. "I'm glad you like her. She's very special to us. She doesn't have many friends, even at school and she pretty much keeps to herself."

"She showed me the view from her balcony and told me it's her favorite place in the world," Sam said. "She also told me about her Grandpa Patrick. I guess he's pretty upset about Caution being gone. He sounds nice too."

"What do you mean, Sam?" Sean's eyebrows furled.

"She told me he comes over whenever he can. He taught her about the constellations and told her about Ireland."

"Sam," Sean began, a little confused. "Patrick is her Great-Great-Grandfather."

"Yes, sir," Sam said.

"He's been dead for almost a hundred years."

"Oh. Well, maybe it's her other grandfather Patrick."

"Sam, I want to ask you something, just between you and

me. Did someone tell you Caution was in trouble?"

Sam took his time answering and began to fidget as he sat in the big chair. "No. Not exactly," he said, not looking at Mr. Murphy.

Sean could tell the young man was getting uncomfortable and didn't want to have him freeze up and stop talking.

"Sam, I've got a little story to tell you. I hope you'll understand. When I was young, maybe a little younger than you are right now, Something happen to me. I owned a bicycle too and I loved to ride it all around. I thought I was fast and a little of a daredevil. Some of my friends who rode bicycles would race and do jumps. I tried following them to show I could do the tricks too but I usually couldn't keep up. One day, a few months later after working hard on my speed, I saw them racing along the edge of a ravine and soon I was right along with them. I was going faster than ever before. I was lost in the speed and the wind, not paying attention to where I was going. I got in front and was beating everyone. There was a big jump coming up and I wanted to show everyone I wasn't afraid. I was getting closer when all of a sudden, this man was standing in my path and I couldn't go around. I was forced to brake and slid sideways, laying the bike down and coming to a stop at his feet. Everyone behind me was forced to stop as well. Everyone started yelling and cussing at me, wanting to know why I stopped like I did. I pointed in the direction of the man and told them I didn't want to hit him. No one understood what I was talking about. There was no man there. I looked back and the man was gone. I got up from the dirt, looking around and didn't see him anywhere. I asked the others where he might have gone, and no one knew what I was talking about. No one saw anything in our path. I went and looked over the hill where the jump was and to my surprise, not only did I not see the man, but a landslide put rocks and boulders in the area where we would have jumped. We would have all been hurt very badly and maybe even worse if we made that jump. That man saved us, but I was the only one who saw him. Everyone else there just said it was dumb luck."

"Did you tell your parents?" Sam asked.

"No," Mr. Murphy said. "I didn't think they would believe me."

"Did you ever find out who the man was?"

Sean got up and walked over and picked up a picture. He handed it to Sam.

"That's my Great-Grandfather Patrick Murphy. When I saw this picture for the first time, I knew the man in the picture was the same one who stopped me and my friends from going over that cliff, possibly saving our lives. I didn't understand it then and I don't understand it now. I just know that somehow, he was able to be there for me."

"Do you think that's who gave me the message?"

"What message, Sam. Did you see someone? Did they

speak to you?" Sean asked with anticipation, going down on one knee beside Sam's chair.

"I didn't see or hear anyone. There was someone or something writing in the fog on my bathroom mirror when I got out of the shower."

"What did it say, Sam? Tell me exactly what it said." Mr. Murphy asked, eyes wide and holding his breath as he waited for the answer.

"It said, 'Caution needs you, find her'. That's why I'm here."

"It didn't say where Caution was or if she was alright?"

"No, sir. Just that she needed me. I thought she was here. I didn't know she was kidnapped."

"And that's all the messages you got?"

"Yes, sir."

"That's amazing," Sean said as he stood.

"Have you seen the man, your great-grandfather, since that day when you were little?"

"I don't think so. Sometimes, I think I see something out of the corner of my eye; a movement, a fuzzy shape, but then there's nothing there, or I get a feeling of someone standing behind me. It could be just my imagination or I'm tired."

"Are you going to tell my grandpa about this?"

"No. I told you I wouldn't. If you want to tell him, that's up to you, but maybe it should be our secret."

"Yours, mine, and Caution's," Sam said with a big grin.

"Exactly. And don't forget, we're still partners," Sean said, holding his hand out.

"That's right," Sam remembered. He stood up and shook Mr. Murphy's hand "Partners."

CHAPTER 42

Now that Quin and Roger were awake and Roger was no longer on the phone, Caution didn't waste any time letting them know she needed to go.

"Excuse me, gentlemen," she said nicely "I really need to go to the bathroom, please."

"The little Miss Darling needs to go to the bathroom," Quin said sarcastically. "Next thing you know, she'll want her dollies and tea service."

"Let up, will you, Quin. Didn't you just have to go, yourself?"

"Yeah, alright. This pain in my arm is making me irritable. I think it's infected."

"Roger went over to the box. "You still have the hood on?"

"Yes, sir. But with the tape on, I can't stand up."

"I'll help you get out," Roger said. "Remember what I said last time?"

"Yes, sir," Caution said. "I'll be good."

Roger lifted her carefully out of the box, placing her feet on the concrete floor. He took a knife from his pocket, opened it, and cut the tape on her ankles and her wrists.

"May I stretch a little first? I got cramped in the box."

"Sure, go ahead, kid. Just keep the hood on and make sure it doesn't accidentally come off, or you're in big trouble with him," Roger said, motioning with his head towards Quin forgetting she couldn't see his gesture. "And you don't want that."

"No, sir," she said, shaking her head inside the hood, still able to understand what he was saying.

Caution began to work her legs and did a few knee bends. She rubbed the areas which were sore and after a few minutes, she said she was ready to go to the restroom. Roger put a hand on her shoulder, guiding her to the door.

"Remember, I'll be right here. And no, I'm not going to look," Roger said with a little laugh.

In the stall, Caution was able to once again lift the hood and take a peek at the outside world through the tall line of windows. It looked cloudy as if it might rain. Without the sun as a guide, it made it look like it was early morning, but without any real way to tell, it could have just as well have been early evening. She thought she would try to find out.

"Are you going to let me have some breakfast this morning? Caution asked. "I am quite hungry."

"Yeah, me too," Roger said. "We'll get you some in a bit, but we have some things to do first."

"Okay. Thank you. I'll be out in just a minute."

"No problem," Roger said.

It was morning, Caution was able to verify. She needed to start keeping a better track of time which may turn into days, if not longer. It might be important.

Caution put the hood back down and exited the stall, once again inching her way towards the sink where she could wash her hands.

"Is there any place I can take a bath?" Caution asked.

"No, I'm afraid not. We'll get you some of those towel wipes to use. You know, like when you go camping. You don't take a bath when you're camping, do you? It wouldn't be real camping then," Roger said.

"I've only done some camping in my back yard," Caution confessed. "I'm not sure I'd like being in the middle of some woods for several days. All the bugs and animals that could eat you. And where would you go to the bathroom?"

"That's why they call it, 'roughing it'", Roger said laughing. "It could get a little rough if you're truly getting back to nature."

"Oh, yuck," Caution said, comprehending what Roger was referring to.

Roger took Caution back to the box. "Sorry, little one, but you have to go back in."

"How long do I have to stay in the box?" Caution asked, trying to be brave and not let her voice crack.

"Till your daddy gives up the gold," Quin said. "And he better make it quick if he wants you back in one piece."

"Quin, shut up," Roger admonished him. "Don't listen to him. He's just messing with you. You'll be home soon. Your father will do what's right.

Roger put the tape back on Caution wrists but not tight and didn't put any around her ankles so she could move a little and not cramp up. He lifted her and put her in the box, not closing the top all the way.

"We'll get you some breakfast in just a little while. What would you like?"

"What? So, you're taking requests now for the little princess? Quin asked. "Well, I feel like a king today. I'd like a T-bone steak with eggs over easy and hash browns. Don't forget the toast." he said sarcastically.

"You can get what you want when we get another vehicle. Until then, you're staying put," Roger said. making a showing of pointing down at the floor. "We can't chance someone saw you leave the van at the burger place. Thanks to you, it probably got towed-in by now or it's in the hands of the cops. You're sure you wiped it down clean?"

Quin gave Roger an angry stare. "I told you I did, and it wasn't my fault something happened to it. Lay off."

There was silence. Neither wanting to say anything to the other. Tensions were slowly growing between the two.

Caution was glad they stopped yelling at each other. It was annoying and hurtful to her ears.

She hoped Grandpa Patrick would come back soon. She always felt better after he visited her at her house. She missed her parents and she wanted to hold and pet Molly. She certainly liked and admired Detective Winston—Vickie, but there was something sad in her eyes; some secret she hid deep inside and wasn't ready to share.

She'd like to have another talk with that boy, Sam. He was fun and interesting. Molly seemed to like him too. *What would he do if he knew she was kidnapped?* she thought to herself.

She closed her eyes, thinking of all those people in her life and wondered if she would ever see them again.

CHAPTER 43

The sea was getting choppy; waves were cresting at about three feet and there was a storm far off in the distance headed their way. There was still a ways to go and John took the ship closer to shore to find a location to dock until it passed over and the water settled a bit.

It wasn't hard to find a place; there were marinas and boat slips all along the coastline. They were able to find an inlet where there was protection from the weather as well as a harbor where they could dock for the night and get some food and rest. George and Frank took their usual turns keeping watch.

"I hope we don't have too many storms pop up like this or we won't get much diving in," Barnes said when they sat at a table in a small bar and seafood grill off the docks.

"It's that time of year," John said. "They could come up suddenly without much warning. We've got a small window to get this accomplished."

"Tell me again what's this got to do with history and a little girl," Barnes asked. "And who's treasure…"

"Ah, hm," John interrupted him when a young lady came up to the table.

"Hi. I'm Sharron. What can I get you folks, tonight?"

Kelly ordered first, going with just a fish sandwich and some fries. She added a lite beer to her order.

John went next. "I'll have a burger and fries with a diet soda. Hold the tomato and onions, please."

"And for you, sweetie?" she asked Barnes, giving him a big smile.

"Just some black coffee, please."

Kelly was watching him, waiting to see if he was going to order a hard drink or a beer.

"Are you sure?" the girl asked cocking her head. "I'm sure a big, strong guy like yourself needs to keep your strength up."

Barnes smiled back, gave a little laugh and said, "Well, I guess you talked me into it. I'll take a burger too. Fully loaded."

"Just like you," Kelly said, not so much under her breath.

John couldn't help but laugh as he hid his face with his hand.

"We'll need to get a couple of to-go orders as well before we leave," Kelly said.

"Sure," the girl said. "Just let me know when you want me to put the order in." She started to head back to the kitchen when she turned and looked back, giving Barnes another smile.

"We can pick you up on the way back if you'd like," Kelly said.

"Trying to get rid of me, already?" Barnes asked. "And

here I thought we shared something special."

"Pa—lease," Kelly said, drawing her shoulders in and shivering. "I may have just lost my appetite."

"Okay, you two," John said. "Listen. We've got to be careful about what we say and who may be listening. I don't want anyone knowing our business." He looked around. There were few people seated and the waitress was in the kitchen. "Here it is in a nutshell. Around 1840, there was an anti-slavery movement being headed by well-established abolitionist and politicians to form a new political party. England was going to secretly help fund this cause with gold being sent over in the form of bullion and coin. The ship it was on sank and it has never been recovered. The movement never got the backing it needed and failed. Two decades later we ended up with the bloodiest war we ever knew; the Civil War.

"Okay. I get it. But what does this have to do with....

"Here are your drinks," the waitress said, placing Kelly's beer in front of her, John's soda with a straw next to him, and then walked around and placed a cup of steaming black coffee in front of Barnes. "That's the way I like my coffee too," she said, getting close enough to slightly rub against him.

"Thank you," he said, once again smiling.

"Yes, thank you," Kelly said, almost dismissively.

John took the paper off his straw and without any thought, tied it in a knot as was his usual habit before placing the straw in a glass of soda. Something he took and kept from an old movie; maybe it was with Carry Grant and involved a cigar wrapper instead of a straw paper, but that's what started it.

When the waitress was gone once again, Barnes took up where he left off. "What's with the little girl? Who is she?"

"It's my benefactor, Sean Murphy's daughter who was kidnapped and is being held for ransom. They want the treasure."

"Well, she doesn't stand a chance," Barnes stated.

"You don't know that," Kelly said, shocked by Barnes' statement. "We could still find it. Maybe save the little girl."

"No. What I'm saying is most kidnapping cases which aren't family related, end up with the person dead or never found."

"I don't want to think about it," John said. "There's no payoff for them if they... if they do something bad to her."

"They won't keep her forever, you know," Barnes said. "I'm just speaking from facts. If they think the cops are getting too close, or there is too much delay in payment, or even if it is made, they might..."

"Enough," John said, nearly too loud. "We have a job to do and we are going to do it, and hopefully, it will help bring her home safe and sound."

"What if we don't find it?" Barnes asked.

"That's not an option," John said. "And I don't want any more 'what if's'. We'll continue this later."

The waitress brought their food. Barnes wasn't smiling at anyone anymore, and they ate in silence.

*

Another boat and its crew were trying to make their way through the same storm. An abundance of care made them find a bay where they could ride it out, but they lost a lot of time and their mission was now in jeopardy.

They would have to get back on the hunt just as soon as it was safe to get out on the open water. Decisions would have to be made soon on what was to come next. Lives and fortunes could be at stake. They were prepared to do whatever it took to make sure they didn't lose the treasure, even if it meant taking some lives.

CHAPTER 44

There was a knock on the metal door and Quin went over and looked out the window. Two men were standing outside.

"It's okay, it's our guys." He opened the small door and spoke with one of them for a minute, then went to the roll-up door and tried to lift it but his arm was too painful. "Hey, help me get this thing up, will you," he said to Roger.

When they got it fully open, a large, dark, four-door car was driven into the warehouse followed on foot by the other man. It stopped just inside. Then the door was closed. The driver got out and tossed the keys to Roger.

"Try not to lose this one," the man snickered, but not in a funny way. "The boss ain't happy." He reached into his pocket and brought out a wad of cash. "This should take care of things for a while. It's full of gas, but don't go for any joy rides. He wants you to sit low till he tells you different."

"How long is that going to be?" Quin asked.

"Till he tells you different," the man repeated.

"We got it," Roger said, giving a disapproving look to Quin. "Thanks."

The man looked over at Quin and his arm. "Man, you need to take care of that before it falls off," he said. "The stuff you wanted is in the back seat and trunk, including those medical supplies. I see why you needed them now." He shook his head and left out the door, getting into another car just outside waiting on him.

"It ain't going to fall off," Quin said. "Is it?"

"Don't be stupid," Roger chastised him. "We'll fix it good as new in a minute. I want to see what all they brought." He headed to the car.

"How come we get stuck doing the babysitting?" Quin asked.

"Because we're showing the boss we can be useful and versatile," Roger said.

"We can be useful and versatile somewhere else," Quin said. "I still want to know why he picked us for this. We're just as good as those guys," he said, giving a head nod in the direction of the door.

"I kind of volunteered us," Roger said, opening the back door of the big land yacht.

"You what?" Quin asked in surprise.

"I thought it would get us in good with him. You know, show he could count on us for bigger stuff."

"Oh, you mean like picking up his laundry, or washing his car?" Quin was starting to raise his voice. "Maybe we could walk his dog next."

"I don't think he has a dog," Roger said bluntly, taking

a box out of the car's trunk containing items he requested.

"That's not the point!" Quin shouted. "The point is we deserve to be respected and treated like everyone else."

"Well, I think this is a pretty big job, myself," Roger said. He put the box on a table and started going through the items. "She could be the key to a whole new future. We were trusted to nab her and keep her on ice till we get the payday."

"She's a kid, for crying out loud," Quin said, shaking his head. "How much trouble is it to snatch up a kid?"

"What does your arm say about it?" Roger said, making his point.

Quin reached for his bandaged arm. "Stupid dog," he said under his breath. "Next time, don't do me no favors by volunteering me till you talk with me. I ain't in no army."

"Here, I ordered you some stuff for your arm. There's gauze and hydrogen peroxide to clean it and mercurochrome so it won't get infected. There's some aspirin for the pain."

"I think it's already infected. It's all red and swollen."

"Well, clean it real good first."

"It'll hurt."

"It hurts now doesn't it? This will make it feel better."

"That's what my mom used to say when I got into scrapes. It still hurt."

"You didn't have anything fall off back then, did you?"

"Stop being a baby. I bet the little girl could take it better than you, unless, of course, you want your arm to fall off. If you don't treat it, it just might."

"Okay, just shut up about it. I'll need some help getting it wrapped up once I get it clean. Give me the bottle of aspirin, I need to take some now."

"There's a case of water in the back seat. Grab a bottle. I'll get one for myself and one for the girl in a minute."

"Did they bring any food? I'm starving."

"Here," Roger said, tossing the keys to Quin. "Check the trunk. There should be a bunch of canned stuff."

Caution was listening to everything being said. She was hoping they would say the name of their 'boss", but it didn't come. By the way they were talking, however, it sounded like they would be staying where they were for a while. She was glad. She didn't want to go to a new place, she was learning more about where she was right now all the time.

She still needed to find a way to let someone know where she was though. She wished Grandpa Patrick could just tell them, but he said it wasn't something he could do. Maybe there was another way. What if…?

CHAPTER 45

Azira Hazar got all the FBI computers and electronic gear set up and talking to each other. All the communications between the main office, the task force, and the field units were in place. He gained access to traffic cameras, ATM cameras, and other outside security cameras in the area Agent Oaks indicated.

He was monitoring police channels and even established a link with certain satellites for real-time, high-resolution, aerial photos; grid searches, traffic problems, and even weather. He didn't think he would tell anyone about the satellites, though. He hacked into the Defense Department to get access. He was fairly sure it was a felony.

Tommy came in to check his progress. "How soon will we be able to…

"Everything is up and running, Agent McGill," Azira said.

"That's bloody impressive. Can we get you anything? A drink or something to eat?"

"Well, if you don't mind. Next time someone is out, can they bring me back a box or two of animal crackers?"

"Animal crackers, you say. Okay, I'll check to see if any of our agents might be by a place that has any of that," Tommy said, giving him a strange look.

The phone for agents to call in to the task force rang and Azira answered.

"Hazar here. Oh, hey, you. Yeah, it's going fine, everything is set up. Yes, he's right here, hold on."

"It's Di—. It's Agent Oaks for you, Agent McGill."

"McGill," Tommy said, after receiving the phone from Azira.

After several minutes of an apparent one-sided conversation, Tommy said "That's another bloody good idea. I see I put the right person out there. I'll keep you posted." Tommy handed the phone back to Azira.

"I want every agent who's not on special assignment to return here for an important briefing in thirty minutes," Tommy said. "After you get in touch with them, I have some real work for you."

There were twenty agents or more crowding the large dining room. Most were afraid they were there to get sad news. But what Tommy said gave them all more hope and something tangible to work on.

"Agent Oaks has come up with another idea. She's heading the surveillance in the area of Jim's Juicy Burgers, so I'm passing this along. As you may recall, that is where we recovered the white van used in the abduction of Caution Murphy. You may also recall there were several bloody bandages found in the first aid kit in the van. This information has not been released to any media, so keep it to yourselves. The driver of the van wore bloody bandages on his left arm where the Murphy's dog, Molly bit the crap out of Caution's abductor.

There was laughter, a few clapped, and a few others made comments praising Molly.

"That's right, good girl, Molly. The man with the bandages might need medical attention. I have our tech, Mr. Hazar doing a check on clinics and hospitals in the area, but most likely, he won't go to any of them. More likely, someone, if not him, will be buying quite a few items from a drug store or a large department type store to treat the nasty wounds Molly gave him. I am also having the tech make a list of all the stores that might carry those type of items in the same area. I want you to canvas the stores on the list which will be divided by sectors and talk with the clerks and if possible, get any security footage they have showing the purchases. Now, I'm not talking about a single box of band-aids or a single bottle of antiseptic. They are going to get a lengthy list of different things to treat these wounds. This is not going to be easy; it's a search for a four-leafed shamrock in a field of shamrocks. So, luck of the bloody Irish to ya. Now get your lists and get out there and call when you think you have something. A little girl is counting on you to help her get home."

After all the agents received their lists and left for their assigned sectors, Tommy went over to Azira. "I have one more job for you if you can do it."

"Sure. Whatever I can do to help."

Tommy handed Azira a piece of paper with some numbers on it. "I need you to locate and track this beacon."

"Okay. I'll need authorization for a Department of Defense satellite connection to get the GPS coordinates for the beacon," Azira said sheepishly."

Tommy smiled. "Just let me know when you find it. Thanks."

CHAPTER 46

After Sam's talk with Mr. Murphy, he, Grandpa Bill, and Vickie went looking for Molly. They already received two calls from police officers related to the BOLO, but both were a different dog. Vickie thought she saw her once, and it was the same breed, but not Molly.

"You don't think she'd try and go back to the farm where she was born, do you?" Vickie put the question up.

"That's not where Caution is," Sam said. "She wants to find Caution."

"He's right," Bill said. "She's going to be following the scent, however faint it might be. I don't know how a dog's nose works, much less, the mind, so I don't know if she is following the scent of Caution, the bad guys, the van, or something else as long as it leads to Caution."

"Molly's smart," Sam said. "Somehow, she'll find where Caution is."

"I bet you're right, "Vickie stated, trying to sound positive and reassure Sam that they will find his friend.

"Caution's smart too. Her Grandpa Patrick was a detective just like you, Grandpa Bill and you, Miss Vickie. I think she said he was a—Pinkleton?"

Vickie couldn't hold the laugh she tried to quickly smother. "Sorry," she said, embarrassed.

"You mean, Pinkerton," Grandpa Bill corrected, also giving a laugh. "That's a very famous detective agency with detectives and private security all over the old west. They're still around today."

They were interrupted as Bill pulled over when a police car with its blue lights and siren activated came up from behind them and went by, closely followed by a firetruck, also screaming out its warnings while it flew down the road in front of them.

Before Bill pulled into the roadway, another firetruck came up behind them and he waited for that one to pass.

"I guess there's a fire somewhere," Vickie said.

"You should really be a detective," Bill joked.

When traffic was clear, Bill pulled out. They hadn't traveled far until they came upon an area where first they could smell the smoke and then they saw the firetrucks parked near a wood and debris pile which was burning and the source of the smoke. A police officer was stopping all traffic.

"At least it's not a house or a business," Vickie said. "I hope no one is injured."

"Just another routine job for the men in red," Bill stated.

"There she is," Sam yelled and pointed towards the front windshield, shoving his arm between Bill and Vickie. Molly was on the side of the road, her nose in the air.

"We're still a long way from where the van was recovered, but this is the way there," Bill said. "I knew she was looking for Caution."

"She was. The smoke is blanketing the area. I think she's lost the faint scent she was following," Vickie said.

Before anyone knew, Sam opened the back door and jumped out running to the dog. "Molly, here girl, come here Molly."

"Sam!" Bill yelled, but to no avail.

Molly was trying to find the familiar sent which would take her to Caution, but she could not find it in all the strange odors covering it up now. She heard a voice calling her name, one that seemed familiar, a friendly voice. She turned and saw Sam, Caution's friend. Here was help to find Caution. She ran to him and jumped around him barking.

"Yes, girl, we're looking for her too. We'll find her, I promise, but you've got to come with us right now. We've got to get you home tonight and then we'll go find her."

Molly knew she wouldn't find Caution on her own now. It would be best to go with Sam. He'll help find her. He's her friend. Molly was truly a smart dog.

CHAPTER 47

South Pass. The place where the waters on the west side now traveled towards the Pacific Ocean. There were many cheers and even a bit of a celebration when the wagon master took his canteen with water from the Atlantic side and poured it into a stream on the Pacific side, mixing the two.

When they made camp, there was a big meeting and the wagon master said there was a decision to be made. Individually, they could choose to head for Fort Bridger where they could get fresh supplies, possibly even fresh animals, and maybe hook up with another wagon train and chance the delay would not set them back for any bad weather ahead, or they could take the Sublett-Greenwood Cutoff.

The cutoff would save them about eighty-five or so miles and a week of traveling time, but there was no water or wood along the forty-mile, desert route. It would be hard on man and livestock and they would try and get it done quickly.

The decision would need to be made in the next couple of days. Many who were wanting to get to the California gold fields as quickly as possible would pick the cutoff route. Many of the Mormons would head to Fort Bridger before going deeper into Utah, possibly to Salt Lake City.

They would camp at the Green River and their wagon master would take the wagons on the cut off while he would choose a leader for those going to Fort Bridger.

Patrick and Mike talked, and it was quickly decided to take the cutoff. They still maintained ample supplies and they would fill up with water at the Green River. They were smart bringing an extra barrel for water. Their oxen were strong, well-fed, and cared for, and Midnight was in good shape as well.

It was especially important to take good care of the animals now. With the hardest part of the journey just ahead, Big Hill was a monster which could suck the life out of animals, and if there was a lot of snow ahead, you could find yourself stuck, waiting for the spring or even the summer to come.

About thirty wagons took the trail to Fort Bridger, most were Mormons. That left forty wagons to continue on the cutoff headed to Soda Springs where there would be another Parting of the Ways. Decisions on which trails to take to California and those who were going to take the trail to Oregon.

It was hard to say goodbye to so many you got to know over the many weeks, knowing you would most likely never see them again, wondering if they would even survive their trip to get to their destination.

*

Near Big Hill was a small trading post manned by a very curious old-timer with remarkable stories and quite a unique nickname. Thomas 'Peg Leg' Smith was a true mountain man, having been a guide, a trapper, a prospector, and even a horse thief, and now, he ran a trading post to help out those on the trail west.

Having been shot in the left leg by a hostile Indian's arrow, it was said when the leg became badly infected, he amputated the leg himself just below the knee before passing out. He was nursed back to health by a friendly Indian woman. Peg-Leg got the name by having a wooden leg he carved for himself while recuperating.

He loved to tell stories about his adventures and all the people he knew and worked with; like John Astor, Kit Carson, Jim Bridger, and Milton Sublette. One of his most famous stories, or possibly the biggest of his tall tales, was about how he completely by accident found and then lost his fortune in gold.

Of course, Mike was captivated with any stories about gold and he listened to every word. Even Patrick found interest is this old man's adventures.

While trying to find a short cut across the desert near Borrego Springs, Peg Leg got lost and climbed a ruggedly high hill to see the surroundings. Near the top of the hill, he noticed some lumps of black ore with yellow specks. The ground was covered with them.

He took some of the ore and finally found his way to California where he got them analyzed. The ore was found to contain pure gold. He tried many times but could never find the same hill where the black ore filled with gold was located.

Peg Leg stated this might be his last year at the trading post as he was going looking for his lost gold one last time.

CHAPTER 48

Early the next morning, the storm passed and there was a beautiful, bright-orange sunrise with multicolored clouds on the horizon. John checked the radar and found the skies clear. The weather report predicted it to be calm all day.

He inspected the boat while Barnes checked and re-secured all the equipment. Kelly fixed a light breakfast while Frank and George got some much-needed rest.

John didn't find any damage or leaks and Barnes reported everything secure and ship-shape. It almost seemed like the conversation from the previous night never happened except everyone was determined to get to their destination as soon as possible and start looking for the shipwreck.

John maps and charts were provided by Sean Murphy for the best possible location of the wreck. There was no guarantee it was anywhere close to where Sean thought it was after so many years of research, obtaining diaries, ships logs, and journals, including the ones of Esther and Patrick Murphy.

This was a ship which was never on any official list of ships making port or leaving a port, nor was it listed as lost in any maritime record. In essence, it was a ghost ship.

John prepared the boat to get underway, and soon they

left the safety of the inlet harbor heading out into the open water. He was happy to have smooth sailing once again. At least, on top of the water. He still wasn't too sure about Kelly and Barnes' feelings towards each other.

He got a satellite phone out of his bag and called Sean to give him a progress report and to see if there was any word on Caution. Agent McGill requested all reports go through him, but John's loyalty to Sean made him the priority. And besides, he was sure there was some kind of communication between him and his agents on the boat and he knew exactly what was going on anyway.

John reported the delay due to the storm, and they would try to make up the time today with the good weather. He was positive the actual search could begin by sometime tomorrow. He learned there was little change in the search for Caution, but felt they were getting closer. There was no need to tell him about Sam showing up at the house and why.

John asked about Mrs. Murphy and Sean told him she was holding her own but still being monitored by her doctor. She was strong and knew everyone was doing all they could. The waiting was getting to all of them.

Kelly came up top as John signed off and gave the report to her and Barnes. She handed him a big Styrofoam cup of coffee and then took one to Barnes.

"There's some biscuits and ham down in the galley. I can

take over here for a bit if you want."

Just as he was about to answer, Barnes started gagging and coughing. He was able to control himself in a few seconds and he looked down into his cup then stared at Kelly. He tossed the contents of the cup into the ocean and crumpled the cup in his hand.

"You trying to poison me, Kelly," he said with a raspy voice.

John looked at Barnes, then to Kelly, and back to Barnes.

"You know I don't take sugar with my coffee. Especially that much sugar."

"Oops," Kelly said. "I guess we all make mistakes."

John knew exactly what she was doing and couldn't help but smile as he turned and made a quick exit down to the galley.

Barnes, still coughing a little wasn't far behind. "Can you believe that girl? What's wrong with her?" he asked, his voice still not normal, tossing the mangled cup at the trash and missing badly.

"You should be glad it was just sugar. There is some rat poison onboard."

"You forgave me, why can't she? I mean, it was a long time ago and it was an accident. I'm a different person. You do forgive me, right?"

John thought about playing this out a bit, but it was too serious. "Of course, I forgive you. I did back then. I even told

Kelly I did. But I can't speak for her now. She was really hurt."

"It's one of the other reasons I changed. I knew it hurt her. I didn't want her to see me like that anymore."

"I didn't want to see you like that anymore and I told you so, I guess it matters more if you have the curves."

"That's not exactly true, well, not at first. I mean, well…" Barnes began to stutter.

"It's okay. I know. I've always known," John said with a sly smile. "Now, don't screw it up anymore."

"What do you mean? She's the one who put a ton of sugar in my coffee. She knows I don't take sugar."

"And here you thought she didn't care," John said, slapping him on the back as he headed back topside.

"Huh?" Barnes muttered, confused, watching John get away without any further explanations.

CHAPTER 49

Big Hill was just that, a big hill. It was the steepest incline they encountered on the entire trail, but just as bad was the descent on the other side.

Most wagon teams could not make it up the steep hill. Wagons would unhitch their teams and a combination of multiple teams and men would take one wagon at a time to the crest of the hill and then return for another.

Before the descent, the wagon wheels would be tied and locked in place. The wagons would be under some semblance of a controlled slide with ropes and stakes being utilized so they would not run away. The total distance they traveled was seven miles and it took them an entire day to get all the wagons up and over safely.

On both sides, they passed the scattered debris of a few wagons which didn't make it so safely. They would break loose, flip, roll, or crash, becoming unusable timber except for firewood. One of the reasons you didn't ride in the wagons on the way up or down or get in its way.

There was no real celebration after getting all the wagons over. Everyone was too tired, and they couldn't afford to waste too much time before hitting the trail again. Every hour wasted could mean days or even lives.

The wagon train received a little luck and there were no cholera related deaths since around Fort Laramie.

Soda Springs was their next major stop. It was quite a sight to see, or rather, taste. There were hundreds of bubbling pools filled with hot, carbonated water naturally formed from ancient volcanic activity. The water tasted just like soda water and was also used for medicinal and bathing purposes as well as getting laundry washed.

The hot pools helped with minor aches and pains, blisters, pulled muscles, and minor stomach problems, but there was a warning about drinking too much and not to let the animals drink too much as the water was alkaline.

Both Patrick and Mike were in much need of a good bath, as were all of the travelers from the wagon trains. Many took their turns bathing in the waters, making many laugh as it bubbled all around them.

There was also plenty of grass and water in the area for the animals and it made for a very refreshing stop.

Just west of Soda Springs was another location where decisions needed to be made. The Oregon Trail headed northwest while the California Trail split into two routes which could be taken. One continued northwest to Fort Hall and then turned southwest to rejoin the main trail again while the other, the new Hudspeth's Cutoff bypassed Fort Hall altogether.

If you were low on supplies or needed fresh animals, Fort Hall would be the trail to take. Fort Hall was being run by the British Hudson Bay Company and was good at having supplies and animals available.

Hudspeth's Cutoff, established in 1849 wasn't any shorter in distance or time, having to cross five mountain ranges, but if you wanted to have better grass on the trail, you could take this trail which went almost due west.

Patrick and Mike decided to take the cutoff bypassing Fort Hall. They believed it was more important to find good grass for the oxen and Midnight. They were very frugal with their supplies, getting more than they needed rather than any real luxuries and resupplying even when they didn't need to. They may have also enjoyed a slight advantage in having the money to start with, courtesy of Patrick's drowned benefactor, the late tailor who left behind his wonderful chest with his gold coins stashed inside.

Gertrude's family, the Burgmann's were going to take the trail to Fort Hall and then continue to Oregon where there was family already settled. Mike found he was truly going to miss her. Other than Patrick and Midnight, she was the only person he regularly talked with, even if neither of them understood everything the other said. He even got used to some of her cooking. The pumpkin pies were still a problem.

It was obvious Gertrude was heartbroken about them

splitting up and it was also hard on Mrs. Burgmann. Mr. Burgmann wanted to talk with Mike before they left.

The night before this new Parting of the Ways, Mr. Burgmann in his one-on-one talk with Mike, offered to let his daughter go with him to California. He even offered to pay him, a dowry of sorts, if they were to get married before they left, and included part of their land when they settled in Oregon.

Mike was shocked, not expecting this development, trying to find the best way to not offend Mr. Burgmann or Gertrude. He wished Patrick was with him. He was better with words than he was.

Mike tried to explain the best he could that they were still unsure where they were going, how far it was going to be, and how rough the trip and the life of a prospector would surely be. It was no life for a young lady. The only way he saw out of this was to tell Mr. Burgmann that if he were to strike it rich, he would try to find them in Oregon, but he couldn't take Gertrude with him. He was not ready to take a wife.

The disappointed father took it hard but seemed to understand, he and his wife only wanting the very best for their daughter.

Gertrude stayed inside the wagon all night, crying. She continued crying as the wagons left for Oregon in the early morning.

CHAPTER 50

They were still in sight of the rocky shore, in an area known to have dangerous rocks. The current and tides were tricky to say the least, even on this beautiful day. John and Frank were running a grid with the side-scanning radar as Kelly kept eyes on the monitor and Barnes steered. George kept his eyes out for any other problems which might arise.

The maps, journals, and descriptions gathered by Sean Murphy gave them a very rough idea where to start their search, but within the vast area of the ocean, this may as well have been a thimble full of water in an Olympic sized swimming pool.

All they could do is wait till they found a reasonable target, send an ROV down to see if there was enough left of it that might match the type and year ship they were after before doing an actual dive. A lot of ifs.

They needed to be careful with the ship and the radar because of the many rocks. Many were just under the surface, only showing themselves during an extra-low tide. Maps helped out some, but nothing was better than watching with your own eyes.

Warning buoys marked some of the areas and there were no other ships or boats in sight except far out to sea.

Kelly, her eyes glued to the radar monitor, didn't see Barnes stealing a glance her way occasionally. She was wearing a light blue top and white shorts which made her golden-tanned legs stand out all the more. A green, pink, and blue mermaid tattoo on her right calf seemed to be smiling at him. Once, he even smiled back, then shook his head and returned to looking ahead for rocks.

Barnes surprised everyone when he came topside that morning clean-shaven. He even trimmed his hair a bit. When John started kidding him about it, he told them it was so the dive mask would fit properly, which was true, but not the only reason.

"I've got something here," Kelly called out.

Barnes slowed the boat, thankful the water was calm at the moment.

John left Frank with the cables to the submerged radar unit and went to the monitor.

"Is it a debris field," John asked, trying to get a view of the screen.

"It's hard to tell," Kelly said, straining at the readout. "There's still a lot of rock and stuff that's making it difficult to tell, but this looked different."

John watched the replay of the pass-by and noted the GPS coordinates.

"Barnes, do a three-sixty from this course for about fifty yards and drop anchor. We'll send the ROV down to take a look. Good catch, Kelly," he said, giving her a high-five.

The side-scanning radar module was retrieved and the remote-controlled ROV was prepared and launched from the diver's platform.

It didn't take long for it to get to the bottom, only about sixty feet down. The onboard camera was sending a good picture back to the boat.

Visibility was about thirty to forty feet as long as it didn't get too close to the bottom, stirring up the sand and sediment.

John was an expert operator of the ROV, having done the exact same thing hundreds of times in many conditions around the world. It allowed him to find many of the treasures he proudly showed off during his exhibits.

Everyone was so busy watching the ocean or the monitor, no one noticed the new, high-tech toy; a high-flying, camera-equipped drone watching them. On another boat just out of sight, another monitor was being watched.

"How long can you keep it up?" Kline asked the crew member with the remote control as she sat sunning herself and drinking a cocktail on the front of the boat. She was wearing a two-piece bathing suit, a big floppy hat, and dark sunglasses.

"Well, uh, about another ten minutes, ma'am" the embarrassed crewman answered. "Then we need to bring it back and change batteries. We have enough batteries charged to keep it up, —eh, —to keep it flying for about four hours with regular changes of the batteries."

"There's nothing happening for a while. Bring it back and reload the batteries and let me know when you're ready to get it back up."

"Yes, ma'am."

"Maybe we'll see what our little patsies have found for us today," Kline said to herself.

CHAPTER 51

Caution was given a can of cold pork and beans with a plastic spoon and a bottle of water. Roger cut the tape around her wrists so she could eat, but she had to stay in the box with the hood on. He did leave the top open.

"It may not be what you wanted, but it's all we got right now," Roger said.

"Thank you," Caution said genuinely. "I'm sure it will be delicious. I'm starved."

"Just let me know when you're done, and I'll take the can."

The small can of pork and beans had a pull top, so a can opener would not be needed. Caution pulled the lid off, licking it clean. She lifted the hood just enough to be able to feed herself. She took the first spoonful and found she was right, it was delicious. She didn't know if it was because she was so hungry, or if pork and beans were actually that good. She didn't ever remember eating them before.

Before she knew it, she was wolfing the entire can down, licking the spoon clean too. She washed them down with the water and she instantly felt better as well.

Although she wasn't exerting herself, she needed the

boost of energy it gave her. Plus, she never knew when or if she would get a chance to run. It was always in the back of her mind, but she needed to make sure if she did, she could get away. There would be no telling what they would do to her if they caught her.

Although Roger seemed a little nicer, even if he did kick Molly, she thinks Quin would hurt her without batting an eye. She was glad Molly bit him.

Roger came back over to the box. "You all done?"

"Yes, sir," Caution said holding up the can with the plastic spoon sitting in it. "May I keep the water; I'm not done with it yet?"

"Yeah, sure," Roger said, taking the can and walking away.

Caution smiled a little under the hood. Roger took the can, but not the lid. Caution hid it under her leg. It still had a bit of a sharp edge which could cut the tape or possibly the box if she needed. She hoped Vickie and Grandpa Patrick would be proud.

Caution heard the big metal roll-up door going up and then heard the engine of a car or van start-up. She could hear the vehicle leave the building and the door come down.

She didn't know if it was Roger or Quin who left. She hoped it was Quin. She didn't want to be left alone with Quin. He didn't like her. The feeling was mutual. Caution kept quiet.

She thought about trying to get out when there was only one of them there, but not if it was Quin. She also thought maybe she should try when they were asleep, but she was scared. Maybe Grandpa Patrick would come back and help her or at least give her some advice or encouragement.

"Hey, little missy, are you awake?"

Caution sighed. It was Quin.

"Yes, sir."

"I hear you like to play games. Would you like to play a game with me?"

Caution wasn't sure if he was being mean or was willing to try and be nice. She bet on the former.

"Let's try a guessing game," Quin said. "Can you guess how many little girls I've killed?"

Quin was showing just how cruel he could be. He was tired, bored, and hurting. A very bad combination if you are babysitting.

Caution wasn't going to fall into his trap. She didn't answer.

"Come on, now, take a guess. Two? Three? Five? Maybe more? Guess what number you're going to be?"

Caution was getting more mad than scared. She almost blurted out something. Even some bad words.

"You're not going to cry now, are you little princess? If you have to cry, just let it out."

Quin went over and kicked the bottom of the box, startling Caution.

"Do you miss your mommy and daddy? That daddy of yours sure has a hard head. He likes to play games too, but you know what? I'm better at those types of games."

Caution bit her lip a little. Now she knew Quin was the mugger who hurt her father. She got even madder, clenching her fists, wanting to use the can lid to hurt him, but she still wouldn't say anything.

"Do you need to go to the bathroom or anything?" Quin deciding to try another tactic to get her to talk, but Caution knew better.

"Have it your way," Quin said, kicking the box one more time for good measure before walking away.

Caution resolved she was going to make Quin pay for hurting father. He was going to jail for a very long time or maybe even worse.

CHAPTER 52

The trek across the Hudspeth's Cutoff was draining. Not much water on the trail and the push to get across the north to south ridges was relentless, taking up nearly any time they would have saved by going the other route. They traveled the nearly twenty-three miles in five days rejoining the main California Trail near what was called the City of Rocks at Cassia Creek.

The rock formations looked like buildings or huts forming a village. This was another place where travelers left their mark, usually with axle grease on the rocks.

They went over nearby Granite Pass, which marked the halfway point to California, going southwest following several creeks and then west to the Humboldt River. This would lead them to the Sierra Nevada's, but first, they would have to endure the Forty Mile Desert in the Humboldt Basin.

This was a long, dry, stretch of sand and salt deep enough to trap wagons and oxen. Water, if any could be found there, was poison and there wouldn't be any usable water until you got to the Carson River. Many did not make it across.

Wagons and contents were abandoned when the animals could no longer pull or even stand, the carcass and the sun-bleached skeletons of horses, mules, and oxen were strewn all the way across. Grave markers were everywhere.

No matter where they were going in California, Patrick and Mike and the rest of their troupe would have to cross this deadly expanse.

Patrick questioned if gold was worth the risk and even Mike wondered if he shouldn't have gone with Gertrude and her family to Oregon instead.

Patrick was worried about Midnight. He was strong and healthy, but should he put the horse through the torture of the desert ahead of them. If he turned him loose, someone might capture him and take him across anyway. He would be needed once they got to California and horses were sure to be expensive, no matter their condition. Plus, he helped save his life. He would have to think hard on this tonight.

Both boys languished through a rough time with everything on their minds during the night, trying to get any semblance of sleep. The trail ahead is what would turn them into men, or ghosts.

CHAPTER 53

The ROV was in the water searching for what was believed to be a possible debris field. Just by the printout, John held in his hand of the side-scanning radar image, they couldn't tell much.

Over a hundred and fifty years of ocean currents, storms, hurricanes, shifting sands, and who knows what else, things got scattered, covered, moved, and destroyed.

The wooden ship could be completely gone, its contents strewn over acres or even miles of the ocean floor, and no remnants of any of its frame or cargo remaining to be found.

John, from many years of experience and resolve, watched patiently, while the others seemed tense and anxious as the ROV searched a grid John set up where they believed Kelly saw something on the monitor.

The ROV, which John called Snoopy, not for the cartoon dog, but because it snooped the ocean floors, held three bright headlamps, a wide-angle and close-up cameras, and a robotic arm at its disposal. It looked a little like a big generator and a small robot conceived a baby. It was a top of the line ROV which Mr. Murphy purchased for John's work not long ago.

George was seated at the helm although the boat was

anchored, engines idling. He cocked his head one way, then the other. He took his sunglasses off, looking around. Then called Frank over, telling him something in his ear.

Frank went to the front of the boat, checked some ropes and the anchor, gave a look around and then came back and gave George a nod.

Frank pushed his sunglasses up on top of his head as he went down to where their bunks were located and returned shortly. Everyone else was glued to the monitor of the ROV.

Suddenly there was a loud blast which startled everyone. Barnes almost hit the deck while John and Kelly jumped up.

"What the hell, Frank," John yelled.

Kelly put her hands over her ears, her eyes were bugged out, and she was shaking like a leaf.

"We were being spied on," Frank said, pulling his sunglasses back down and then opening the breach of the scoped rifle he held in his hands, ejecting a spent cartridge. "There was a drone overhead. It's been permanently neutralized."

George was quickly up on top scanning the sea for any boats in the area. This close to shore there were several, but none were close enough for him to get a look on board.

Kelly, still shaking returned to the monitor just in time to see the ROV pass over something which did not look like a rock.

"John, stop. You just passed something."

"What was it?"

"I don't know, but it's worth looking at again."

John maneuvered Snoopy back around to where Kelly indicated.

"It was right there," Kelly insisted.

John was working the controls and got Snoopy turned around. He slowed it down and kept watch on the monitor.

Barnes, still shook up over the gunshot, looked first at Frank, then at George and asked him if it was safe.

George just gave a slight smile and stated, "It's safe."

"There," Kelly almost yelled, coming out of her seat a few inches.

John brought the ROV to as close to a hover as he could with the underwater currents still giving the ROV a back and forth movement and let the camera get a good shot.

"What is that?" Barnes asked.

"It's part of a wooden ship," John said, laughing. It's the stern and part of a rudder of a mid-nineteenth century ship. It looks like most of it might be buried.

"How can you tell how old it is just by that small part?" Barnes asked.

"It's an old sailing ship. There's no screws."

"You mean propellers?" Kelly asked.

"That's correct," Barnes said. "In the Navy, the proper term for a modern ship's screw is screw propeller."

"Let's just call them screws, then," giving Barnes a sour

look.

"You can call them whatever you want, sweetheart," Barnes quipped.

"Don't call me that, you…"

"Okay," John said. "We've got time for one dive, maybe two if we hurry.

"Who's going down?" Kelly asked.

"Ha." Barnes let out a quick laugh.

"Don't get your hopes up, putz," Kelly returned

"What'd I say?" Barnes held his hands up.

"You and me, Kelly, will take the first dive," John said. "We'll see after that. George, Frank. Keep an eye on things here up top. I don't know who they are, but I think It's obvious what they want. They shouldn't make any moves until it's confirmed we've found the right target."

"No problem," George said.

Frank just nodded his head.

"There's no other boats close, so I wouldn't put any diver's flags out, but they probably already know."

John and Kelly got their wetsuits, weight belts and tanks on. They each carried large flashlights with them. They got to the edge of the diver's platform and Frank, who was dressed in a wetsuit himself just in case of an emergency below, helped them get their flippers on.

John pulled his mask down and adjusted it. "Com check,"

he said.

"Loud and clear," Barnes stated.

Kelly pulled her mask down and did a com check as well.

"Too loud, too often," Barnes came back.

She gave Barnes the finger just as she jumped in.

John was right behind her.

Divers in the water," Barnes called out. "Com check," Barnes asked once more.

"Loud and clear," John reported.

"Loud and clear," Kelly reported

"Let me know when you reach the bottom," Barnes stated.

"Will do," John said in between loud breaths.

"It's beautiful down here," Kelly said between her own breaths.

"It always is," John said.

They followed the ROV lines down, deciding not to bring it up yet. They could use its headlamps to help locate items.

"We've touched bottom," John said in just a few minutes.

"One small step for man," Barnes repeated the familiar phrase.

They began checking the area and within about fifteen minutes, John called out to Kelly.

"I think I see something over to our right," he said.

Kelly swam in that direction, keeping no more than ten

feet from John. "I see it!" she exclaimed. "This must be it." Her excitement was registering in the quickness of her breaths.

"Hey, guys," John said to the crew up top. "I think we have," loud breaths "a wooden ship of the kind we are looking for."

"Great news," Barnes returned. "Can you confirm it is the right ship?"

Everyone topside was waiting for the good news.

"Not at this time," John said. "There's not much of it here. The currents have scattered much of it around."

"Is there any way to be able to confirm it's the right ship?" Barnes asked.

"Only if we find what we're here for," John said with another loud breath following.

"Can you tell how big the debris field is?" Barnes asked.

"No. Visibility is now only twenty feet or so," John said. "We'll need the metal detectors on the next dive."

"I hope this is it," Barnes said. "I honestly do want that little girl to be safe."

"We're coming up. We'll let the ROV's do some more work for us," John said.

"Got it. Divers surfacing," he called out.

John and Kelly were helped getting into the boat from the diver's platform, getting their masks off.

"This could be it, couldn't it? Kelly said excitedly.

"It's possible, but a lot of ships have gone down in this area," John said. He gave a long pause. "But yes, this could be it," he smiled.

William N. Gilmore

CHAPTER 54

Bill, Vickie, and Sam brought Molly back to her home where she, of course, ran around looking for Caution.

"Thank you so much for bringing her home," Mrs. Murphy said.

"Yes, thank you," Sean said. "All of you."

"It's our pleasure," Bill said. "I think we were right, and she was trying to track Caution, but the scent vanished because of a fire and smoke in the path she was taking. Maybe we can try tomorrow after we all get some rest. It's getting late and I need to get Sam back to his mother."

Molly came running back into the main room and started to dance around Sam. He reached down to pet her, but she backed away and barked. She then began to go in circles and started to run off. When Sam didn't follow, she repeated everything.

"Bill, it's getting late like you said, why don't you and Sam and you too, Vickie, stay here tonight. We have plenty of room as you can see and Vickie, I wanted to talk with you about our arrangement, if you don't mind."

"Can we, Grandpa Bill.? We can get a quicker start with Molly tomorrow."

As if on cue, Molly barked and started going in circles around Sam again.

"See, she wants me to help her find Caution, Grandpa. I know it. I need to help her."

"We can come back tomorrow and start where she left off," Bill said.

"I don't think that's it, grandpa. She might try and run off again on her own. She'll stay with me, I'm sure."

Bill looked over at Vickie who gave him her 'Don't ask me,' face.

"I don't know Sam. We've got to get Vickie home. We need to get cleaned up and eat and I would have to try and explain to your mom.

"We have a great service which can take care of your clothes tonight," Mrs. Murphy said. "And we have plenty to eat. I would appreciate you staying, especially if Sam thinks he can help with Molly. By the time you get him fed and home, and you get home yourself, it will be so very late. Please reconsider.

"Please, Grandpa Bill."

Bill gave a big sigh. "If Vickie says it's okay then I'll call your mother. If she says it's okay…

Sam went and grabbed his grandpa, giving him a big hug. Then he turned and said "Thank you, Mr. and Mrs. Murphy. I know tomorrow, we'll find Caution with Molly's help."

"I think you just might," Mr. Murphy said.

"That would be so wonderful,' Mrs. Murphy added, a little crack in her voice. "Let me show you to your rooms," she offered.

Sam was given a room next to Caution's and Bill was next door to him.

Vickie was given a room on the other side of Caution's.

All the rooms were like five-star hotel suites with huge beds and overstuffed pillows as well as their very own large bathrooms with walk-in showers and soaker tubs.

Bill made the call to his daughter trying to explain everything.to her, but she stopped him in the middle telling him that as long as Sam was with him, it was fine with her. He was relieved he did not have to go into everything.

A special laundry and dry-cleaning service arrived and promised to have all their clothing returned within the hour. They brought a special truck with all the facilities to do the work right there in the driveway. Meanwhile, they provided everyone with beautiful white robes and house shoes. It must be nice to be super rich.

Bill never had a shower with twelve shower heads shooting water from every direction. He may have stayed in it a little too long.

Everyone was invited to join for a meal in the auxiliary dining room after they were finished cleaning up.

Meanwhile, Molly laid at the foot of the bed waiting as

Sam finished his shower and put on the robe and slippers. As they were leaving the room Sam was given, they passed Caution's room.

Molly went up to the door and started to paw at the door; it opened slightly.

"She's not in there, girl," Sam said. "Let's go downstairs. I think they're waiting on us."

Molly pushed the door with her muzzle, opening it wider and made her way into the room.

"Molly," Sam called from the hallway, but Molly didn't come out.

Sam pushed the door open a little wider, peeking inside and calling for Molly in a whisper before he went all the way into the room. The reflected light of the full moon was shining through the balcony doors, bathing the room in a soft glow.

Molly was by the doors, sitting, looking out.

"Come, Molly. We need to go downstairs."

Molly continued to sit, looking out, cocking her head.

"Come on, girl, this is Caution's bedroom and she's not here. I don't think I should be in here without her knowing it. Molly, please." Sam slowly walked over to the dog, venturing to take a look out himself. "It is beautiful," he said mesmerized. "I see why she likes it so much," he said to Molly.

Molly looked up at Sam and pawed the balcony door.

"No girl. I don't think that's a good idea," Sam said

shaking his head. "If you were to run off now, I think everyone would be mad at me"

Molly pawed the door again and Sam reluctantly grabbed the door handle.

"Please don't run off," Sam begged.

He opened the door and Molly ran out and went straight to the railing and jumped up with her front paws so she could see over the top.

"Good girl, Molly." Sam walked out onto the balcony beside Molly, rubbing her head and looking up to see the moon and the stars.

The wind was blowing, rustling through the trees and bushes. Sam lifted his head letting the wind caress his face as it did the first time he was on the balcony with Caution. The wind was flowing through his thick hair, sweeping it back and forth once again. The air smelled sweet and clean. A tear began to form as he thought about Caution and what she must be going through and how he wished she could be there.

"I can see why this is her favorite place in the whole world," Sam said again to Molly, wondering if she understood as he rubbed the back of his hand over his wet eye.

She jumped down and went over by the railing and sat, looking up as if she were looking at something beside her.

"It's mine too, when Caution is here, that is."

Sam turned, expecting to see Caution's father, Sean

Murphy, embarrassed that he would be caught in Caution's room without being invited.

Instead, he saw a different man standing at the railing, looking up at the sky. He wore an old English style bowler hat and a long coat. He looked familiar.

After a few seconds, he remembered. It was the man from the picture Mr. Murphy showed him. The man who saved him and his friends from going over the cliff on their bicycles when he was young.

The man turned and faced him.

"Hello, Sam. I'm Caution's grandfather. I'm Patrick Murphy. She needs your help."

Thank you, and please return to witness the continuing adventures of Caution, Sam, Patrick, and Mike in:

Caution in the Wind

Book Three: The Rescuers

by

William N. Gilmore

Coming Soon.

Made in the
USA
Lexington, KY